PARTRIDGE IN A BEAR TREE

RENAISSANCE SHIFTERS
BOOK TWO

MURPHY LAWLESS

MKP

PARTRIDGE IN A BEAR TREE

ISBN-13 (e-book): 978-1-83557-035-7
ISBN-13 (print): 978-1-83557-036-4

Cover Artist: Malice & Mayhem Book Covers

CHAPTER 1

Ashley Torben's fated mate was at the far end of the bar, drinking a pale ale and being the cutest girl Ashley had ever laid eyes on. She was a petite redhead, *so* curvy, with a big braying laugh and an appealing, swaggering confidence. She vibrated energy and no-nonsense and enthusiasm, chatting easily with the people around her and obviously comfortable in her own skin.

The idea of talking to her terrified Ashley beyond comprehension.

It's fine. Her bear, the world's most patient sow, spoke gently, and Ashley nodded complete agreement. It was, in fact, fine. Better than fine. It would be wonderful. Perfect. Amazing. That was how fated mates worked.

She still couldn't get her feet to scoot even a single inch across the floor.

This was full-on disaster lesbian behavior and she

knew it. This was "we moved in together six months ago but I'm not sure if we're dating" territory. It was fully in the "we smooch and snuggle all the time but I don't know if she's into me" zone. She could *not* be wrong about this, not with the sudden, heart-striking certainty of fate on her side. Not with her bear's quiet calm reassuring her that the tiny redhead down the bar was everything Ashley had been looking for in a partner.

And yet the very thought of approaching Penny Partridge struck paralyzing fear into Ashley's heart. What if fate was *wrong* this time? What if Penny screamed and ran away, or worse, just wanted to be friends? What if she wasn't interested in dating women? What if—

Somebody crashed into her from behind, swore, and muttered, "Sorry, Ash, it's a madhouse in here."

Ashley, knocked loose from her helpless, longing gaze toward her fated mate, turned to give her cousin Jon a sympathetic look. "It's nuts. I had no idea the crush would keep up a whole week after the gigs."

Jon, a big stupidly handsome guy like all her cousins were, gestured with an entire beer-glass-laden tray at the group of women near the far end of the bar. The group that contained Penny, and, incidentally, two other members of the actual rock band she was a part of. "As long as the Sixty Pix keep hanging out, people are going to keep flocking to see them, even if they're not playing. I mean, *Emma Hart.*" He dropped his voice into a whisper, which would have made him absolutely impossible to hear if it weren't for the fact that Ashley, like most shifters, had exceptional hearing.

"She's Gwen Booker now," Ashley muttered. "She has been the whole time we've known her."

"*Yeah*," Jon agreed, "except she's *Emma Hart*. And it was *Emma Hart*'s dad who was arrested in our parking lot. And it's *Emma Hart* who is Bill's fated ma—"

"Now that's not true," Ashley said more crisply, if still quietly. She took a moment to glance down the bar again, where Gwen Booker, Actual Rock Star, was elbowing Penny, Actual Rock Band Drummer, and laughing over something. "Emma was her stage name, and, like, Emma was a blonde tweenager who got super famous, and Gwen is her real name and is a grown-up noirette—" Well, Gwen had dyed black hair, but close enough— "and he met her as Gwen and had no idea she was Emma, so it's definitely Gwen who's his mate. Don't be stupid about it, Jon. It's not her fault she's famous."

Her cousin eyed her. Ashley blew her cheeks out, exasperated. "It's not. She was a kid when she got really famous doing tv and stuff. You've heard her talk about it. Her parents pushed her into it, and she quit when things got bad."

"And now she's gotten herself famous again by being a rock star," Jon pointed out.

"Yeah, but that's as Gwen! It's also not her fault the media's screeching about the whole childhood fame thing! Anyway, don't be weird about Bill's mate.

That's…weird." Ashley wrinkled her nose, and Jon snorted with laughter.

"Good thing Bill hired you as the general manager and not a copy writer. And I'm not the one being weird."

Ashley froze. "What are you talking about?"

"You've barely gone near Gwen all week! You seemed okay when she first got here, but you got really weird as soon as the rest of the band showed up. I know *I* had a crush on Emma Hart when I was about eight, but I didn't know you did!"

"I'm not not going near Gwen!" Ashley said indignantly. "Gwen's great! Get back to work!"

Jon laughed and bumped his shoulder against hers, still without upsetting the tray of mostly-empty beer glasses he was carrying. "Great rebuttal there, cuz. You're definitely not being weird. Or starstruck. Or anything like that." He slithered past her and went behind the bar to drop the empty glasses off. Ashley leaned against the bar itself, hunching her shoulders and glaring at the grain of the its surface.

She wasn't being weird *or* starstruck. It was just that Penny was with Gwen a lot of the time, and Ashley couldn't manage to say anything coherent to the drummer, so it was safer to avoid the situation entirely.

You'll have a very hard time wooing your mate that way, her bear said patiently.

I can't woo her anyway if I can't even talk to her! Ashley risked a glance down the bar. Gwen and the third member of their band who hadn't yet left town, Sandy, were still down there, but Penny had disappeared. Ashley scowled after Jon, squared her shoulders, and worked her way through the crowd at the bar to go say hi to Gwen. That would show her stupid cousin. And after that she had to get back to work, because she had real plans for the Thunder Bear Brewpub, and none of them involved mooning over an adorable redhead. They also didn't involve counting on Gwen's band, the Sixty Pix, to bring in the crowds for the rest of eternity, even if it had been a great promotional event over the past week.

"There you are!" Gwen grabbed Ashley into a hug as she finally made it through the throngs of people filling the bar. "I've hardly seen you all week. Bill's got you crazy busy, huh? How's being the new general manager? Or, what did he say he was going to give you as a job title? Queen And Mistress Of All The World?"

"We went with 'General Manager,'" Ashley said sheepishly.

We are not a sheep, her bear told her firmly. *You may speak bearishly, but not sheepishly.*

Ashley opened her mouth, about to argue with the bear out loud, then clicked her jaw shut again. 'Bearishly' suggested she was a grumpy gus, but her sow would be offended at the idea that she might be, by nature, surly. And to be fair to the bear, it was not an ill-tempered creature at all. It was patient, mild, thoughtful, and gentle, which weren't words usually associated with bears, but then, shifter bears weren't like true bears.

"As long as he gave you the raise that should go along with the Queen And Mistress title, I'm good with that," Gwen said airily.

"Ooh, Queen And Mistress," said a bright voice at Ashley's elbow, and beers began to materialize as Penny made a space for herself in the little grouping. "I like that. One beer for you, G. One for Sandy, and one for you, Queen And Mistress Of The World." Penny handed Ashley what was clearly meant to be her own beer, since she only had three of them.

Ashley, politely but with determination, said, "Oh, no, I couldn't possibly, that's yours, and besides, I've drunk more Thunder Blunder than I could possibly need in one lifetime," and firmly but gently pressed the tall glass of beer back into Penny's hands.

At least, that's what happened in her head. What happened outside her head, out there in the real world where everybody else was a participant too, was that she said, "Oh no I'm already blunder drunk for a lifetime," and shoved the beer away in a panic, splashing most of it down Penny's shirt.

CHAPTER 2

It had been a perfect opportunity, Penny thought, and then it had all gone wrong.

There was Ashley Torben, amazonian beauty, six feet tall if she was an inch, *finally* overcoming what was apparently an unholy terror of Gwen Booker and dropping by to say hi. Penny understood that terror, honestly: she'd been tongue-tied and shaking with nerves the first time she'd met Gwen and recognized her as child star Emma Hart. But she'd overcome it brazenly enough that they'd been in a band together for almost two years before Gwen found out that Penny *had* recognized her. The point was, Penny got it. Meeting superstars was kind of a lot.

Although how Ashley, with her incredible cheekbones and deliciously full mouth and big soft eyes could possibly be overwhelmed by anybody, Penny didn't know. Ashley looked like the kind of woman people would stop on the street to smile after, or maybe mistake for a supermodel, or maybe offer them-selves as personal servants for the rest of eternity just to spend some time with her. She was so tall. Slim. Strong arms that could sling beer trays around effort-lessly. Jeans that she really knew how to wear.

Penny might, she admitted to herself, be nursing a *terrible* crush on the new pub manager. All she needed to do was be able to *talk* to the woman and find out whether Ashley might be interested, too. So Ashley finally coming over to say hello was the opportunity Penny needed, and the fact that she only had three beers—one for herself, Gwen, and Sandy, the band's second singer—was not an obstacle. Penny was more than willing to sacrifice her own beer as a way to chat Ashley up.

She had not, however, planned to sacrifice it down her shirt.

Penny couldn't help the shriek as beer flew out of the glass and over her her clothes. Her shoulders caved in, like she could avoid getting soaked that way, but mostly that just provided a space right between her boobs for the beer to funnel down. Her shriek turned into a giggle, then another shriek as beer reached her belly button and soaked the waistband of her jeans. "Cold! Sticky!"

Gwen, languidly, said, "Hot and sticky is better," underneath poor Ashley's spluttered sounds of horror and apology.

Shoulders still hunched, Penny said, "One time," first to the beer soaking her shirt, then to Ashley's incredibly apologetic deep brown eyes, "one time I'd just gotten a glass of milk, and as I turned away from the fridge, the entire bottom fell out of the glass."

Ashley blinked at her in frantic confusion, continuing to make small, squeaking apologetic noises. Penny nodded and went on. "The whole bottom. I don't know how it was constructed that the bottom could fall out like that, but it did. It was one of those 'time slows down' moments, and I saw fluid mechanics in motion. The middle of the milk blooped—up, I think, it's been ages since it happened—and then blooped back down and I could see the middle of the column drop with individual droplets rising and forming and falling around it. It was genuinely incredible. And then it all hit the floor in a giant splat, obviously."

She looked down at her shirt again. "This was almost *exactly* like that. Except foamy. But I could actually see the whole wave of beer just rising up there, cresting, collapsing, like it was in slow motion. *Sploosh.* Nothing I could do to stop it."

"I am *so sorry,*" Ashley interrupted shrilly.

Penny had the impulse to give Ashley a hug, although given that she was covered in beer, she was fairly confident Ashley wouldn't actually appreciate that. "It's okay. Seriously." She offered a hopeful smile. "I'm not going to melt, and I wasn't wearing my seven thousand dollar leather Prada jacket, so—"

Ashley, faintly, said, "Oh my God," as Gwen said, "You don't *have* a seven thousand dollar Prada jacket," in exasperation. Ashley looked back and forth between Penny and the singer, eyes wide with confused dismay, and Penny, in the most reasonable tone she could manage, said, "Which explains why I wasn't wearing it, doesn't it? Honestly, Ashley, it's okay. It's just beer. I'm going to go wash my shirt out, but it's fine, okay?"

"Come back to the staff bathroom," Ashley whispered. "I can get you a brewery t-shirt to wear."

"Oh!" Penny brightened. "That'd be great. I was thinking, at least I'm not wearing a white shirt, but yeah, that'd be great, thank you!"

"It's the least I can do," the tall woman said, still in a whisper. "Come on, this way."

Ashley turned to elbow her way through the crowd. Penny followed after her, grateful that people actually got out of her way. Even in heels, she was at least eight inches shorter than Ashley, and had spent a lifetime squirming through the small spaces between people instead of just brazening it out and expecting people to move. Mostly because no matter how brazen she was, she was also still barely over five feet tall. She muttered, "Bane of my existence."

There was no reasonable way Ashley could have heard that through the noise in the bar, but the tall blonde cast her a stricken look anyway. "I really am sorry."

"Oh, I wasn't talking about you!" Penny said, startled, as Ashley pushed open the staff door and gestured her through. "I was talking about being short. Oh, wow, it's so much quieter in here." She managed to lower her voice by the end of that, although she'd started out very loud. "Uh, sorry, I didn't mean to be shouting at you."

"You're not short, you're—" Ashley broke off as Penny gave a loud, disbelieving snort.

"So speaketh the Amazon. You're what, six feet?"

"Six one," Ashley said almost apologetically. "Here, this is the staff bathroom. I'll get you a t-shirt."

"Six one! I'm five two! Look at this!" Penny toed her boots off and stood flat-footed on the tile floor, something she absolutely would not have done in a more public bathroom. Hands on her hips, she glared up at Ashley, then gestured wildly at the difference in their heights.

Ashley Torben visibly bit the inside of her cheek, trying to keep from laughing, the effort making her warm skin tones absolutely glow. Her mane of dark blonde hair was tied in half a casual up-do, keeping it out of her dark eyes and away from her broad, strong cheekbones, although a few tendrils, tucked behind her ears, fell to frame her square jaw. "Okay," she said in a voice obviously still fighting laughter, "okay, you're kind of tiny. I was going to say it looks good on you."

"But now you've seen the truth of the matter, which is that if I take my shoes off, I actually disappear like a bug," Penny said with a dramatic sigh. "Like I said, bane of my existence. Do you wear heels?"

Ashley, startled, glanced at her own feet. "Hardly ever. Not because of the towering over people thing, because I do that anyway. They're just not very comfortable." She brightened. "I have an amazing pair of clogs that have like three-inch platform soles made of cork and I *love* those. They're not heels, but they're tall shoes, at least."

"All my shoes are tall," Penny agreed. She put hers back on—they were clogs, too, actually, and had somehow been spared the beer that had dripped down a lot of her front—and went to the sink to strip her shirt off and stare at the reflection of her bra in dismay. Most of the cups were stained a darker berry red than their usual shade. "It's a nice color. Too bad about the beer smell."

"I am *so sorry!*" Ashley fled, presumably to get a t-shirt.

Penny yelled, "It's fine! Accidents happen!" after her. The bra came off for a thorough rinsing and a scrub with soap from the dispenser, although she paused to put her beer-wet shirt back so she wouldn't jiggle quite as much while she scrubbed. Ashley came back with a shirt clutched in her hands and offered it silently. Penny shook her head. "I'll wait until I've washed this, at least. That way I'm not splashing water all over the new shirt. Thanks. You don't have to wait for me," she added ruefully. "I know you've just taken over managing the place and I'm sure you've got better things to do than watch people wash bras in your bath-room sink. Think the hand dryer has enough power to dry this thing?" She lifted the dripping bra.

"It's lace," Ashley said in a funny voice. "Not padded cups. It might."

"Are you a padded-cups girl? I can never get them to

fit right." Penny squeezed as much water as she could out of the lace and squished it out of thin padding around the underwires before draping the bra over the hand dryer and stripping her beery shirt back off to plunge it into the sink.

"Sorry!" Ashley spun around to fix her gaze on the bathroom door.

Penny laughed, though a trill of disappointment went through her. Apparently Ashley was either too polite, or too disinterested, to ogle. Not that Penny generally wanted to be ogled, but if it was Ashley ogling, she would make an exception. "Yeah, because you've never seen boobs before, and nobody's ever seen mine. It's fine. I promise, after being in a band for ten years, I've gotten really comfortable with randos seeing my boobs. Not that you're a rando! It's just, you know, backstage and stuff! I'm going to stop talking now!" Maybe if she drained the sink, it would suck her down into it and she wouldn't have to face having made a complete—well, tit—of herself in front of the Thunder Bear Bar manager.

Ashley coughed like she was trying to cover a laugh. "Want me to try drying your bra?"

"That would be great," Penny mumbled. "I've almost got the shirt clean, I think, but it's going to take forever to dry. No, wait, don't you have work to do?"

The other woman was already putting Penny's bra under the dryer, which kicked on with enthusiasm. Ashley raised her voice to say, "They can hold down the fort without me for fifteen minutes. You can probably dry off with some of the paper towels. I really am sorry. I'm not usually clumsy."

"I don't usually try to thrust beers on unsuspecting women in bars, either, so I think we can say we're both at fault."

There was an audible pause. "Do you thrust them at suspecting women?"

"I wouldn't say *thrust*," Penny said in an attempt at dignity. "And I'd prefer to say I offered them to *interested* women, not suspecting ones. That makes me sound like they have reason to be suspicious of me. Okay, is it too weird to hang my shirt up in front of the window or something?" She'd wrung it out, and was now eyeing the small, open bathroom window near the ceiling.

"I kind of want to see you try."

Penny sniffed. "I'll have you know we short people have our ways. They involve turning the garbage can over and climbing on it, if necessary."

"Or asking tall people to reach it for you." Ashley smiled over her shoulder at Penny, realized she still didn't have a shirt on, and turned pink along her magnificent cheekbones. "Er, sorry."

"I shall spare you the terrible vision of my naked flesh and put a shirt on," Penny promised, and did so. The Thunder Bear Brewery had a pretty good icon, a big grizzly-type bear with a slash of stylized lightning that stretched across her boobs in an appealing way. "Better?"

Ashley glanced at her again, expression sheepish. "I

just don't want to be rude. I think the bra's drying. The underwires might take a while, though."

Penny shuddered. "Nothing worse than damp underwires. Okay, there are lots of things worse than damp underwires, but in the moment, you know?" She ended up flinging her shirt over the top of one of the two stalls in the bathroom, mostly because it would be up against the wall at the window and it could dangle across the stall bar. "Somebody is going to get dripped on because of that, aren't they?"

"There are two stalls," Ashley pointed out. "If they're either desperate or dumb enough to use the one with the wet clothes hanging over it, they won't mind a few drips. Do you want to feel this?"

"My hands are all wet and wrinkly. I don't know if I'll be able to tell if it's dry." Penny took some paper towels and dried her hands, then felt the bra carefully. "Underwire is definitely still wet. The lace is pretty good, though. I can wear it if I have to. Yay me for lace bras."

"I don't know how you wear them. They itch." Ashley shuddered.

"People always say that, but it's never bothered me. But I can wear wool against my skin, too."

Ashley twitched so hard it was almost a jump. "Really? Augh! I can't even think about it without itching!"

Penny, without exactly thinking it through, said, "Well, if you've got an itch, I'll scratch it," then heard what she'd said and laughed out loud. "I mean, um. That didn't come out the way I meant it."

"Hahaha no I'm sure it didn't." Ashley actually just about *said* 'hahaha,' it was so staccato and fake and clearly uncomfortable. "I think I just heard something out there that needs my help sorry bye!" She thrust the bra back at Penny, and hurried out of the bathroom.

"Okay," Penny said into the silence, and to her damp bra, "that went well. Oh, no, wait, it was the other thing. *Not* well. Dang. No, that's fine. I didn't need a tall, hot, blonde girlfriend anyway. Just a dry bra and a rock and roll tour. There will be *tons* of hot babes on tour," she promised the bra, and finished drying it.

CHAPTER 3

hy did you run? Ashley's bear asked plaintively as Ashley bolted down the hallway. *Someone to scratch our itches would be nice. I like back scratches.* The bear dreamed up an image of vigorously rubbing its spine against a tree.

We can go for a hike in the morning and scratch our back on a nice tree, Ashley promised desperately.

But Penny will scratch it for us! And she's our mate!

That's not what 'if you've got an itch, I'll scratch it' means in human terms, Ashley whispered.

Her bear stared at her.

Ashley lowered her head into her hands a moment before bracing herself to go into the bar. The bear's silent confusion was more than she could imagine trying to clear up right then. *Just trust me, okay? I'll explain later. There's work to do right now.* She pushed the staff door open, going back into the loud, crowded bar where she could be distracted by people, work, and music instead of thinking about either her bear, or Penny Partridge.

Of the two of those things, the bear was easier to ignore. Penny came back into the bar several minutes later, wearing what must have been a fairly dry bra by then, and the t-shirt Ashley had given her. She managed to catch Ash's eye, gave a shimmy to show off her shirt, and beamed at her before going back to Gwen and Stacy. Ashley was still distracted by the effects of that shimmy when another of her cousins, Laurie, who looked almost exactly like his brother Jon, stepped into her line of sight. "Did you just dump a beer all over one of the Sixty Pix?"

Ashley sighed. "Yes. On Penny. Accidentally."

"Too bad I didn't get it on video. We'd have gone viral. Could you do it again? Oh! And she's wearing one of the pub's shirts now. That would be perfect."

"I am not deliberately pouring a beer on someone, Laurie!"

"Well, what if I did, then? You can film it. I bet she'd reshare it and we'd definitely go viral."

"Laurie!"

Her cousin sighed and went back to work, muttering, "Fine, but I'm telling you we're missing an opportunity here," over his shoulder at her.

"I can live with that!" Ashley snapped after him. "I have a lot of other things to do anyway!" Things that could conceivably keep Ashley busy for the rest of her life, thus removing the opportunity to ever really talk to Penny.

We can't never talk to our mate. Her bear, usually so calm, sounded actively distressed at the thought.

Ashley exhaled noisily. *I know. I'll nerve myself up soon, but she does keep coming over here in the evenings, when I'm crazy busy. Just let me get through the weekend, and Monday, when it's calmer, I'll really* **talk** *to her, all right?*

All right. The bear settled back down, placated, and Ashley promised herself she wouldn't disappoint the animal. Monday, after all, wasn't all that far away.

PENNY WAS GONE ON MONDAY.

Bill, Ashley's oldest cousin, mooped into the pub early Monday afternoon and slumped in one of the booths, looking out the window with the most forlorn, pathetic expression Ashley had ever seen on his face. She slid into the booth across from him, worried. "What's wrong?"

"Gwen had to go back to Denver," Bill said despondently. "She and the others got everything worked out with Mike Piccolo's production company over the weekend, and once that was done none of them could put off going back to their day jobs any more."

A cold fist of horror seized Ashley's heart. "Wait, what? Penny's gone too? And Sandy?" she added, trying to cover her tracks. As if it was important to hide the fact that she was crushing on the drummer, never mind that Penny was actually her fated mate. But it was important to keep it quiet, in its way. She wanted to spend time getting to know Penny before dragging her into the whole mess of her massive, bear-shifting family.

"And Gemma and Myles left last week. I'm supposed to go into Denver this weekend to see Gwen, but..." Bill sighed heavily and sank farther into the booth seat. "Two weeks ago I never really thought I'd find my mate, Ash, and now that I've spent ten days with her all I want to do is lie on my face and be sad because she's not here. It's very manly of me."

Despite the frantic hammering of her own heart, Ashley couldn't help a little laugh as she reached out to her cousin, who grabbed her hand for a moment. "I think it's pretty manly to admit you're sad without her. Even your pompadour is drooping."

Bill released her hand to check his hair, which wasn't really drooping, but the fact he checked made Ashley smile. He was one of four brothers, and he claimed the pompadour was how he distinguished himself from his look-alike brothers. The truth was that Jon and Laurie were both a bit smaller and long-haired, and Steve, the brother who had left a few years ago, had always been less theatrical in appearance than the other three. Ashley was pretty sure Bill just liked having fancy hair. Having reassured himself the pompadour was still in full form, he slumped again. "I knew she was going to have to leave, obviously. It just sucks that she actually had to leave."

"So you guys are going to work this out long-distance?" Ashley asked tentatively.

"Well, that's why you're taking over management of the pub. Part of it, at least. The brewery needs less day to day supervision, so I can travel with her some. But yeah." Bill shook his head. "I guess I always thought finding a mate would mean settling down into a traditional lifestyle. It never occurred to me that it might mean uprooting my whole life, instead."

Ashley swallowed. "Is that what you want?"

Her cousin took a deep breath and let it out slowly, obviously giving her question some real consideration. "Honestly, Ash, it's hard to say right now. I've been so snowed under by managing the pub and the brewery that I don't think I've known what *I* wanted for a really long time now. You and Gwen really kind of kicked me in the butt about that and made me realize it, so..." Bill's eyebrows drew down, although he smiled. "So if I didn't say so, thank you."

"Oh. You're welcome. I don't think I meant to do anything helpful like that."

Bill's smile turned to a quick laugh. "You succeeded despite yourself, then. But to answer your question, I don't *not* want to uproot things. I'm still figuring myself out right now, I think. I want to travel with Gwen, for sure. I could never ask her to stop being a bonafide *rock star*, so if one of us is going to change our lives, it has to be me."

Ashley laughed, too. "She was a rock musician until last week, Bill. The whole rock *star* thing is new, I think. You're both going through a lot of lifestyle changes right now."

"Yeah, okay, you're not wrong, but you know what I mean, right? If we're going to be together, it'll be between her gigs, or with me going to where she is. And no, it's not what I expected, but yeah, it's what I want, because it's what'll make it work for *us*."

"What if…" Ashley shivered, thinking about Penny's sparkling brown eyes and her quick, loud laugh. "I mean, what if you really didn't want to go on tour with her? What if what you really wanted was just to be right here, doing the thing you loved doing?"

"She's my mate, Ash. If fate is for real, and it sure feels like it is, then I guess if that's what I really wanted, then that's what would work for us."

"Even if it meant not being together all the time?" Ashley hadn't even realized she had any of these questions, but now, talking to her cousin, she was starting to think it wasn't just Disaster Lesbian-ing that had kept her away from Penny the past week. She obviously had deep personal concerns—she wouldn't call them *fears*, dammit—that had made approaching the redheaded drummer seem genuinely impossible, no matter what fate was telling her.

"We're already not going to be together all the time," Bill pointed out philosophically. "I *do* have the brewery to run, and Gwen's going to be running her ass off doing gigs for the next year while they hype the new album. She's talking about moving out here to Renaissance, but her bandmates live in Denver. If they want to practice when they're not on the road, either everybody's going to have to move out here or somebody's going to have some insanely long drives for rehearsals, and getting four near-strangers to move two hundred miles so I can be with my girlfriend whenever she's home is a big ask."

"So you don't think you're moving to Denver," Ashley said cautiously.

Bill shrugged, palms up. "Not right now, for sure, and honestly I hate the idea in general. But I've got to believe fate means something, and we'll work it out. How are you doing?" he asked, in less of a subject change than he imagined. "I know you've only been managing the pub for a week, and it's been a crazy, crazy week, so on a scale of one to ten, how overwhelmed are you?"

"Oh, about a seventeen." Ashley laughed shakily, then shrugged. "No, not that bad. Eight, maybe? It's not like you were doing a bad job, Bill. It's just that you were juggling too much. And between Oktoberfest and the Sixty Pix blowing up the airwaves this past week, business has been booming. Now that both of those things are over...well, I guess the real work begins now."

Her cousin leaned forward, arms folded on the table. "We haven't talked much since you took over, and I know that's mostly my fault. I've been with Gwen the whole time. But you said you had a vision for the brewpub, Ash. You want to talk about that?"

"The past week and the band have helped launch us

in the direction I want to go in," Ashley admitted. She gestured around the warm, clean pub, which had more people in for lunch than they usually did. "A younger clientele, for one thing. No disrespect to your parents, but the jazz evenings and soft rock Muzak weren't exactly calling out to the young and hip."

Bill grinned. "Because the young say 'hip,' just like we Millennials do."

Ashley grinned back. "Yeah, exactly. So there's that, just aiming for a younger clientele, but also, look, what's one thing that this town really lacks, Bill?"

His eyebrows rose. "I feel like the list could go on for quite a while and yours probably doesn't include an excellent adult ball pit, so you tell me."

"A ball pit? Really?" Ashley blinked at her cousin, who ducked his head.

"It was the first thing that leaped to mind. Go on, what are you thinking?"

"I was thinking Renaissance needs a good gay bar, or at least somewhere that's an obviously queer-friendly space!"

"Oh." Bill wheezed laughter. "Yeah, I can see why that might be more useful than a ball pit. That seems like a good idea, Ash," he said more seriously. "It's not something I'd really thought about, but it'd probably be not only popular locally but could get skiers in during the winter, and even faire people in the summer. Although there's already a lot of beer at the faire."

"Tons, but the faire closes at seven and the pub is open until two," Ashley said with a smile. "That's a lot of time to mosey into town and have dinner and some drinks. Same with the ski resorts in the winter. Most of the skiing shuts down by four or five in the afternoon because it gets too dark. Having a queer destination in town could bring in a bigger clientele. I'm not planning to throw the whole cozy log cabin vibe out or anything. I just want to make it clear, visually and in advertising, that this is a safe space for queer people to come enjoy themselves."

Bill spread his hands. "It's your party, cuz. Go for it."

CHAPTER 4

The worst, and possibly best, thing about leaving Renaissance, Colorado behind was that it meant Penny wasn't mooning over Ashley Torben at what was a clearly-defined arm's length distance. She was under the impression that generally speaking, Ashley was in to girls, but given the way the tall brewhouse manager had avoided even looking at her while she was standing around the bathroom half naked, Penny had to assume that Ashley wasn't specifically into *her*. And Ashley's smile had been pained when Penny had tried to show off the Thunder Bear Brewery t-shirt she'd been loaned, "So, yeah," Penny breathed to herself. She hadn't thrown away her shot, it just hadn't hit. These things happened. It didn't matter all that much.

Which was why she was still moping about it two weeks later. Penny smirked and did a drum roll that made Gwen look up from tuning her guitar. "Are you still pouting over Ashley blowing you off?"

"No!" Penny smashed the cymbals to emphasize the sincerity of her response, then grabbed them to stop the reverberations and glanced guiltily toward the studio doors. "Maybe."

Gemma, their keyboardist, snorted inelegantly. "Totally. And if you don't stop making noise they're going to throw us off the show before we get to perform."

"They're really not." Myles, on bass, was sprawled on the studio floor like they weren't about to do a live performance on Denver's most popular radio station. "Even if they wanted to throw the rest of us out, they really want Gwen on the show, and she won't be on it without us, so we could set the microphones on fire and they'd still welcome us with open arms."

"Probably not if we set the microphones on fire," Gwen disagreed. "They'd have to call the fire department. It'd be a big mess. And I think one arrest in the band's proximity is enough for the time being."

Penny exchanged glances with Sandy, second guitar and backup singer, who grimaced and said, "Yeah, but it wasn't one of *us* who got arrested."

"There but for the grace of God, though." Gwen flexed her hand and wrist like she was remembering the impact of punching her ne'er-do-well father in the nose. He'd tried to press charges, but the fact that she'd hit him after he showed up back in her life almost twenty years after running off with her childhood fortune had made the judge laugh in his face. The same judge had also refused him bail, on the extremely valid argument that he was obviously a flight risk, having run off once before. Penny hoped he rotted in jail for the rest of his miserable life.

A soft crackling sound alerted the band as the DJ, a woman named Keely, flicked a speaker on between the rooms. Even Myles got up, and Sandy shook herself, taking a deep breath in preparation as Keely spoke. "Ready to rock? Countdown will go from thirty up there on the screen while we introduce you, and then you're live. You have seven minutes of air time before we have to take a commercial break, and while we're doing that we'll move the whole band from the sound studio in here with me. We good?"

Gwen cast a quick grin around at the band and said, "We're good," with easy confidence. Keely had explained that all to them at least two times before, but Penny imagined people screwed up a lot and the repetition was the DJ's best way of minimizing mistakes. Keely gave them a thumbs-up through the window and a countdown light flicked on above it as Gwen turned her attention to Sandy. "Just like we always do, Sandra Dee. A cappella chorus for our intro."

Sandy wrinkled her nose affectionately at the nickname, but nodded while Penny marveled at Gwen's calm. Performing for live audiences was old hat, but Gwen was the only one in the band with any real experience with performing on air or for a studio audience. The lead singer lifted a hand, counting down with her fingers as the clock reached the last few seconds. Sandy fastened her gaze on Gwen, not the clock itself, and her alto voice, deep enough to be a tenor, soared out effortlessly as Gwen's fist closed on a zero.

They hadn't planned for their song *Not Again* to begin with a chorus, but after Gwen had debuted it as the encore for a free gig a few weeks ago, their fans had embraced it as their way to call the band on stage. None of the Sixty Pix were dumb enough to look a gift horse in the mouth: if the fans wanted the song that way, then they'd by gum get it. The band had added the chorus-first version of the song, both as a live recording and a new studio recording, to the album when they'd dropped it in the wake of their unexpectedly successful weekend playing at the Thunder Bear Brewpub in Renaissance.

Gemma came in on the keys after Sandy brought the guitar in, with Myles and Penny following with the bass and drums just a few measures later. Gwen, with her powerful lead vocals, waited to join them until the first verse, and Penny got a glimpse of the DJ beaming in her booth, eyes bright as the song soared. There was no transition when they finished it and moved into *Midnight Kiss*, an older song that had been their biggest success up until the new album's release.

It was totally different playing for a visible audience of one, even though Penny knew there were thousands of people listening to the airwaves, and even though they'd practiced and recorded the songs in-studio. They rarely got to see the effect of their efforts on one individual person, but Keely was absolutely beaming as the band poured into her booth and took their seats after their performance was done. "I have to wait to gush until we're on the air," she whispered, "but oh. my. *God*!"

That set everybody at ease, and the next twenty minutes flew by as the band fielded questions about where they'd come from, what their hopes were, and where they were playing next. The DJ did ask Gwen about her history as a child star, but Gwen leaned into the line Penny had used when they'd decided they were going to try to break big: the Sixty Pix were a band that looked forward, not back. Keely accepted that gracefully, and the rest of the interview went incredibly well.

Not all of them did, over the next month. Gwen had warned the rest of the band over and over again that there would be people who would insist on dragging her childhood stardom into interviews, that she'd be the focus of attention, and that she was worried about the friction it might cause among the band members. But they were adults, not the teens and tweens Gwen had been friends with the first time she'd come to fame, which made a huge difference. Everyone knew how to handle themselves.

Besides, their keyboardist, Gemma, who was possibly the bluntest person Penny had ever met, made that clear during an increasingly-disastrous interview near the end of their pre-holidays promotional tour. The show's host kept pressing Gwen about the situation with her horrible father until Gemma got up, physically placed herself between the interviewer and Gwen, and in an incredibly flat tone, said, "Would you like to talk about your senior prom, Delilah?"

The woman paled so much Penny thought she might actually pass out. As she gaped, Gemma said, "Then why don't we stick to the topics we agreed on beforehand," and continued to stand there, a blockade between Gwen and the invasive questions, until Delilah nodded and returned, shakily, to less dangerous grounds.

Afterward, Gemma only shrugged and said, "Toldja we had your back, babe," and left it to her boyfriend, Myles, to later admit that Gemma had been doing recon on every single person they were scheduled to interview with, just in case she needed ammunition to keep interviewers from haranguing Gwen.

"It turns out Gemma's terrifying when she wants to be," he said in apparent astonishment, while the rest of the band dissolved into disbelieving laughter and teasing him about never having noticed that before. Gwen had gone off to find Gemma afterward, though, and they'd come back having clearly had a good cry. The whole thing made Penny's heart want to explode with happiness. They'd been together for a long time, and worked hard to get where they were. Finding out they could probably withstand the rise of unexpected fame wasn't a surprise, but it was a relief.

Penny just wished she had somebody to share it with. Gwen had her new boyfriend, Bill, who mostly wasn't traveling with them, but to whom she was sending pics and texts and video clips all the time, and Gemma and Myles had been together forever. Sandy regarded the entire spectrum of romance and sexuality as something amusingly appalling, and of no personal interest, but Penny…

…was *not* daydreaming over tall gorgeous Ashley Torben any time her mind drifted. The only reason Ashley, specifically, was on her mind was that she was Bill's cousin, so Penny was reminded of her every time Gwen talked to or mentioned her paramour. That was it. Simple proximity reminder, nothing more. Not Ashley's broad smile or her slightly worried expression as she watched over the pub she was managing, or the way she raked her hand through her thick blonde hair. Penny would have been obsessed over some other beautiful blonde if it hadn't been for that. A Hemsworth brother, for example.

Although she had to admit Ashley was probably a more likely romantic option than any of the Hemsworths, due to that same proximity problem. Even if Ashley *wasn't* interested, she was still probably a more likely romantic possibility than a Hemsworth.

Penny, amused at herself, decided to stop worrying about it, and immediately went to find Gwen and say, "Do you know the Hemsworths? You know, from back when you were famous? Or, I mean, can you get to them?"

Gwen was, at the moment, sprawled on a deck chair despite the fact that Denver weather was grey and promising snow. She opened one eye, then the other, and snickered. "First, 'can I get to them' sounds vaguely threatening. Second, no, I don't know them. Third, are you trying to distract yourself from thinking about Bill's cousin again?"

"You cannot *possibly* know that." A blush climbed Penny's cheeks, totally betraying her attempted denial. "How did you know? She's so *pretty*."

Gwen sat up with an out-loud laugh. She was the polar opposite of Ashley, physically: very pale, dyed black hair, ragged jeans and cut-up t-shirts under leather jackets, stompy boots and scarlet lipstick. Although, like Ashley, she *was* tall. Not *that* tall, but from Penny's vantage, pretty much everyone was tall. Gwen swung her legs over the deck chair and grinned up at Penny. "So we're not crushing on Luke, then."

Penny's eyes widened and her blush heated up even more as she realized she'd totally betrayed herself. She sat in the other chair with a *thunk* and put her face in her hands, mumbling, "No. I didn't even know he had a cousin named Luke."

"I think he may have a cousin with every name you can imagine. There seem to be dozens of them. Buuu-ut," Gwen said, sing-song, "there were only three female Torbens around when we were there, and one of them was Bill's mom, so that leaves Ashley and… Cassidy, I think. There are a lot of them," she added in a mumble. "But Cassidy was kind of quiet. Luke was the very, very blonde guy."

"Oh, him," Penny said dismissively. "Too pretty. Ashley didn't even notice me, though."

Gwen reached over to pull Penny's hands away from her face. "Want me to ask Bill if that's really true?"

"Oh my god, what are we, five? My friends talk to your friends?"

Gwen grinned and sang a couple more lines of the song it reminded them both of, then shook her head. "All right, then, new cunning plan. Come to Renaissance with me for the holidays."

"Are you nuts? For one thing, we're touring, like, all over the place through the holidays!"

"Unless Mike pulls out some kind of amazing last-minute publicity coup, we're not traveling anywhere between the twenty-first and the thirty-first, and we're performing *in* Renaissance on New Year's Eve. Gemma and Myles are going up to Vancouver to spend the holidays with their families, and Sandy's going to Mexico with her crew like she does every year. Usually it's you and me in Denver at Christmas anyway. Why not make it Renaissance instead?"

"Because I don't want to be a weird stalker chick if she's not into me?"

"If she's not into you," Gwen pointed out, "there are like seventy-three other Torben cousins to make a play for. You can regard it as your own personal Torbasbord."

Penny stared at her. "Just for that I'm going to wreak absolute havoc with the entire Torben clan. I will wreck relationships. I will shame your name. I will be the leading tabloid material for badly-behaved band members for months."

Gwen cackled. "No, you won't. And if you do, then oh no, they'll stop asking me about what it was like to be Emma freaking Hart. Win-win for me!"

"Dang it! Outplayed!" Penny threw herself backward in the deck chair, theatrically and without considering the fact she was sitting on it crosswise. She hit the deck on the far side, her knees and calves still on the chair, wheezing as she tried to draw air back into her lungs. Gwen squeaked with alarm, and after a couple of seconds, appeared over the edge of the chair, gazing down at Penny with worried eyebrows.

Penny, trying to scrape together the remains of her dignity, said, "Yes, I believe I'll join you in Renaissance for the holidays," in the calmest, most collected tones she had at her disposal. Then, in despair, she added, "*Because apparently I'll accidentally kill myself if left alone without adult supervision,*" as Gwen, treacherous BFF that she was, dissolved into gales of laughter.

CHAPTER 5

*S*ure, Ashley thought somewhere just shy of Christmas, *go for it, cuz. No problem. You've got this aaaaalllllll under control.* Christmas was around the corner, and two months of managing the Thunder Bear Brewpub had been…

"*Challenging,*" Ashley said beneath her breath, rather than choose one of any number of *other* words she would have liked to describe the situation.

She'd known going in that it was going to be work, but Ashley wasn't afraid of hard work. There was a good crew working at the brewpub, and the one guy who didn't like the idea of taking the pub in a queer-friendly direction had quit when she'd called a staff meeting and explained her vision. They were better off without him, and she knew it, but it still stung.

Everybody else had been comfortable with it, and the only significant visual change around the pub were the

Pride flags that now hung on the walls along with the traditional American and Colorado state flags. Ashley was anticipating a lot of fun during Pride the following year, but that was months away, and they had plenty of groundwork to lay first. Aside from that, the biggest change was auditory: her aunt and uncle, who had started both the brewery and the pub, were really into jazz and easy listening styles of music. Gwen Booker's explosive entrance into the Renaissance music scene had turned the pub into a rock-and-roll destination overnight, and Ashley was more than happy to lean into it.

She just wished her wretched *cousins* would take their jobs at the pub more seriously.

Ashley had known—Bill had mentioned, and she'd seen it herself—that neither Jon nor Laurie, the two youngest Torben brothers on that branch of the family, were particular self-starters. Not when it came to the pub: they were both great at the Renaissance faires they spent half the year working, but they both seemed to regard the rest of the year, and their jobs at the actual pub, as sort of…voluntary. Oh, they did what they were asked. Bill had made that clear, but they didn't do much they weren't specifically asked to.

After six weeks of that, Ashley was both amazed Bill had lasted four years trying to run herd on them, and that he hadn't killed them. It was now less than a week until Christmas, and if she had to *tell* them to pick up the slack one more time, Ashley was fairly certain her head was going to explode.

Her poor bear gave her a distressed look. *Maybe we should sleep.*

"Can't sleep, clowns will eat me," Ashley breathed. The bear felt even more worried, and Ashley sighed. "No, clowns aren't going to eat me, but I'm afraid hibernating isn't really an option. I'm going to have to Talk to them."

Even the bear could hear the capital letter in 'talk.' It gave the impression of nodding solemnly before providing an image of a sow swatting a couple of unruly cubs with a big paw.

Ashley chuckled. "Yeah. Just like that." She went into the staff office, which was small and dark and, she realized in that moment, rather comfortingly den-like. Maybe she could just curl up under the desk and sleep through Christmas.

We're not fat enough, her bear informed her mournfully. *We'd have to get up to eat.*

"Oh well. It was a nice thought."

"What's a nice thought?" Laurie, the youngest and possibly prettiest of her pub-owning Torben cousins, came into the office a few steps behind her. His long, sandy blonde hair was back in intricate, elf-like braids, and his smile was infectious as he threw himself into one of the uncomfortable office chairs. "And what can I do ya for? I'm supposed to be over at the leather-working shop in half an hour for the next class, so I've only got a minute."

A flare of real anger sparked in Ashley's chest and

she had to take a deep breath to quell it. "You're *supposed* to be on shift this evening, Laurie."

He waved a hand gracefully. "Jon said he'd cover it for me."

"Jon is already supposed to be working tonight," Ashley said through her teeth. "He's large, but he's not two people."

"Oh, it'll be fine. If I don't get this class finished I'm not going to have the new garb ready for March—"

"We have a holiday party with eighty guests in the event room tonight, Laurie!"

Her cousin blinked at her. "Don't we have extra staff on for that?"

"You and Jon *are* the extra staff!"

Laurie eyed her. "Is this about our beef, Ash? Is that why you're freaking out?"

"Our—" Ashley broke off, bewildered, then groaned. "*No*, you twit, it's not about your dumb 'beef' thing that isn't even real. This is about you and Jon—"

"Did I hear somebody taking my name in vain?" Jon came in just as Ashley was building up a head of steam, and whistled at his brother. "Lookit you with the fancy braids." Like Laurie, he wore his hair long, although his was loose right now, and a darker blonde than his brother's. Otherwise, they looked stunningly alike, even to Ashley, who'd grown up with them and knew they weren't twins. Laurie's features were finer, his jaw a bit slimmer, and Jon's voice was a solid octave deeper, but they were made from the same mold.

Laurie tossed his elf braids, looking smug. "It's

gonna be part of my new character for Faire. Which is why I need to finish the leather-working class, Ash—"

"Do you two understand you actually *work* for the pub? That you get paid? That you're expected to show up and fulfill your shifts?"

Jon dropped into the other office chair with an expression that might, if Ashley was generous, be considered faintly guilty. "Well, yeah, of course, but—"

"No, Jon, there's no 'but' after that." Ashley took another deep breath. "Look, I love you two, but you need to listen to me, okay? I get that the faire season is a lot more fun than a nightly shift in a bar, but neither of you two take the off-season part of your jobs seriously. If you're scheduled, you're expected to show up. Bill spent years covering your asses—"

Both the brothers looked offended. Ashley raised her palm, cutting them both off. "He did. He worked shifts you didn't show up for. He did a lot of detail work you should have seen and done yourself. He—"

Laurie burst out with, "We help out when we're asked—"

A sound erupted from Ashley's chest. Not a sound she would have let herself make if there had been any true humans nearby, but there were three shifters in the room and the door was closed, so she didn't modulate the startlingly deep roar that broke through Laurie's protest. Laurie and Jon both straightened, wide-eyed, and Ashley could see Laurie just about bristling, as if he might go so far as to shift in the middle of the office. "You help out *when you're asked*," she agreed strenuously, before he could object any more. "But you're both grown adults who have been working at this pub since you were old enough to serve beer, and at the faires since well before that. You're perfectly willing to pick up slack at the faires. I've seen you do it thousands of times. If something needs doing there, you do it. I expect you to do the same damn thing at the pub!"

Jon, still sounding more guilty than Laurie did, said, "But Bill—" and Ashley interrupted with another of those near-roars.

"*Bill* worked himself to exhaustion because he was the only one doing the job around here! He expected you to pull your own weight and when you didn't, instead of confronting you about it, he just did everything you weren't. *He* expected you to behave like responsible human beings, because he knew you *could* do it, but neither of you ever bothered. You only do the minimum around here, and that's part of why the pub damn near went under!"

A little to Ashley's surprise, that shut both her cousins up. They exchanged glances before Jon said, "The pub what? But we're doing really well?"

Ashley looked upward like she would gain strength from the ceiling beams, then mashed her lips flat as she stared at her cousins. "Are you serious right now?"

"Are *you* serious?" Laurie's voice rose. "The pub nearly went *under*? Why the hell didn't Bill say anything? Why do you know that and we don't? That can't be right!"

"Would you have listened?" Ashley asked softly. "Bill asked for help over and over again, guys."

"Not that kind of help! Not 'the pub is going under' help! He—" Laurie broke off as Jon cast him an uncertain look, and, less confidently, said, "He never said he needed *that* kind of help."

"Because every time he asked you for any help at all, you did exactly what you were asked to do and nothing else. Your brother was doing two peoples' jobs, Laurie. *Both* your parents used to run this place and the brewery. When they retired Bill picked it all up by himself. He hired me—"

"Because he found his mate and wanted to be able to spend time together!" Laurie said.

Ashley sighed. "Because he needed somebody else to manage the pub. Finding Gwen is probably the best thing that ever happened to him, if for no other reason than it gave him some perspective on that. You two are incredible at running a pub. You do an amazing job of it six months out of the year, all over the country, during the Ren Faire season. But as soon as the season is over, you come home and spend the rest of your time screwing around and doing whatever the hell you feel like instead of helping out around here. And now that *I'm* running this place, you're either going to shape up or ship out."

Laurie's jaw fell open. "You're *firing* us?"

Ashley smiled thinly. "I'm putting you on an employee probation plan. If you don't start taking your jobs here more seriously, then yes, you'll be let go."

"But Mom and Dad *own* this place!"

Ashley stared at the youngest Torben cousin. "Then that would be embarrassing and awkward for everybody, wouldn't it?"

"Jon, she can't—" Laurie shot a look at his brother, decided maybe he wasn't going to get as much support there as he thought, and flushed angrily. "Fine. I'll call Miguel over at the leather shop and see if I can squeeze into the Saturday morning class, if that won't interfere with your schedule for me," he snapped at Ashley, then rose and stalked out of the office.

Ashley tried not to flinch as the door slammed shut. Her bear glared after Laurie. *You should swat him for real.*

If we weren't in a pub surrounded by humans...

"Has it really been that bad?" Jon asked quietly. He'd barely said a word, or maybe hardly gotten one in edgewise, but his deep voice was apologetic and worried. "Have *we* really been that bad?"

"Yes." There was no sugar-coating it, and even if it had been possible, Ashley was too mad right now to try. "On both counts, yes."

"I didn't know." Jon leaned forward in his chair, studying his hands. "Probably because I didn't want to know, or bother to. I know the brewery is doing well. It didn't occur to me the pub might be in trouble. Bill's so..."

"Responsible," Ashley said shortly.

"Yeah." Jon looked up. "I'm sorry, Ash. I'll do better. And I'll apologize to Bill. I didn't mean to...you're right, though. I take the Faire stuff really seriously because it's how I see myself, me and Laurie both, I guess, as helping out. Advertising, making people aware of Thunder Bear Brewery, getting new contacts, all of that. But I do totally think of the rest of the year as my time off, time to get all the detail work ready for next year's Faire circuits, and that my job here is just helping out, not really work. I didn't *know* I thought about it that way until you just pointed it out, but I totally do. I just—" He hesitated, holding the hiss sound in his teeth. "I wish Bill had said something earlier. I get why you didn't. You were waiting to see if we'd shape up once somebody else was managing the place. And we didn't. You must be really disappointed in us."

"I am. You two are closer to my age than anyone else in this family." In fact, Ashley was sandwiched between the two youngest Torbens, nine months younger than Jon and nine months older than Laurie. "We were the Three Musketeers when we were kids."

Jon laughed, a quick quiet sound. "Literally. I actually found those costumes again earlier this year. We were pretty cute. No wonder we were so popular at the Faires. But you kind of outgrew the whole Faire thing."

"I didn't outgrow it, Jon. I just didn't have a family business to fall back on during the off season, so I couldn't dedicate half my year, or even just my summers, to it anymore. You guys still have that, so, you know, don't screw it up. The pub's doing better after the boost from Gwen's band, but I don't have time to hold your hands, and you're thirty years old.

Nobody should have to be holding your hand to walk you through your job."

"Yeah. You're right. And, again, I'm sorry. I'll do better," Jon said again. "Laurie probably will too."

"Don't make promises for him, or pick up his slack," Ashley warned. "Just…yeah. Do better." She sighed. "It really would be embarrassing to have to explain to Aunt Heather and Uncle Pete why I fired their two youngest sons from the pub they own, so don't put me in that position, okay?"

"I won't. Things will change, Ash, I promise. You won't believe how smoothly things are going to go from now on." Jon gave her a hopeful smile that Ashley couldn't help returning, and she sat there at her desk a minute once he'd left. Maybe he was right. Maybe things would turn around. She thought she might let herself believe that, at least for a little while.

"Yeah," she said aloud, mostly to her bear as she readied herself to get back to work. "Yeah, things are gonna go smoothly for a while."

Feeling confident, at least for the moment, she walked back out of the office, and right into Penny Partridge, her fated mate, and proof that things were *not* going to go so smoothly after all.

CHAPTER 6

To Penny's absolute dismay, Ashley was every bit as gorgeous as she'd remembered. It was easy to tell, from having run into her. Almost literally run into her, which, well, technically, Penny *had* been looking for her, and was heading for the staff hallway where she one hundred percent didn't belong, but she hadn't expected to meet Ashley coming out the door. Penny squeaked and stepped back apologetically, then thrust the t-shirt she held in both hands at Ashley. "I brought your shirt back!"

Honestly, Ashley looked dismayed to see her, although the dismay faded into confusion, and then a laugh. "You didn't need to do that. It's yours."

Penny knew that. It had been an excuse to come talk to the tall blonde pub manager. Now that the excuse was gone, she had no idea what to say except, "Oh. Sorry."

Ashley's laugh faded into a smile. "No, it's fine. That

was a nice thought. But it's not like I can sell it now that it's been worn, and it wouldn't fit me, so I can't take it myself. Hi."

"Hi." Penny tried not to sound, or look, drippy with admiration. "I'm, uh, I'm back. I came back with Gwen. For Christmas. If that's okay."

"Why wouldn't it be okay?"

"I don't know. Because last time I was here I threw a beer on you."

"You tried giving me a beer." Ashley's smile grew wider. "I threw it on *you*."

"I mean—well—yes, but—if I hadn't tried giving it to you—"

"Penny," Ashley said in a warm, stern voice, "I am not going to let you take the blame for me dumping a beer on you. And even if I wanted the shirt back, you've been wearing it on all your TV interviews and I couldn't buy that kind of advertising for the pub, so if you're feeling guilty for some reason, how about we call it even?"

Her voice was low and inviting and completely mesmerizing. She could have been suggesting they eat live snakes and Penny would have said, "Uh-huh, okay," agreeably. "Wait, you've been watching our interviews?"

To her surprise, color crept up Ashley's cheeks. "Sure. Everybody has. Everybody here kind of thinks you're Renaissance's own home-grown band now, I think."

Penny blinked. "But we're from Denver."

"Denver has plenty of bands. Give us this one. We discovered you."

They were still standing in the staff hall doorway. They were still standing very close together in the staff hall doorway, and Ashley Torben smelled *delicious*. Some kind of outdoorsy scent, plus malt. It made Penny want to lick her, or stick her nose in the taller woman's…neck. She said, "Okay," still very agreeably. "Please don't ask me to eat a live snake."

"Th—what?!"

Penny buried her face in the t-shirt she was carrying, and, muffled, said, "You have a nice voice and I was just thinking I'd probably agree to anything you said just so I could keep listening to you. Which sounds increasingly awful as I say it. It's one thing to be like, I could listen to a movie star read a phone book. It seems much less charming to say it about a real person."

Ashley laughed out loud and pulled Penny into the staff hall, closing the door against all the sound in the pub. "Movie stars are real people. Remember your friend Gwen was one?"

"She was a TV star, really," Penny whispered, but looked up. Ashley no longer looked at all dismayed to see her. The pub manager had a soft, funny smile, almost wistful, although she shook it off as Penny said, "You know what I mean, though."

"Yeah, I do. Do you want to listen to me read a phone book?"

Penny's eyebrows drew down. "Do you even have

one? I mean, that's really retro. I don't think I've seen one since I was about eight."

"I'm prepared to go to great lengths to acquire one if necessary," Ashley replied solemnly. "Although I'm sure there are other equally boring things I could read to you. The pub's tax returns, for example. A grocery list. The dictionary. No one's ever said I had a nice voice before. I don't want to waste the opportunity."

"I bet," Penny said unwisely, "that I could find something *much* better than a phone book for you to read."

"Really." There was a pause. A *pause.* A Significant Pause. Ashley stared down at Penny during that Pause, and something dark and a little wicked came into her eyes. Then, like she was very much throwing caution to the wind, she put a hand on the wall above Penny's head and leaned in. "What would be better than reading a phone book?"

"Muuagh. Uh. Um. I. A, uh." Penny wet her lips and swallowed. She'd forgotten how to talk. With effort, she scraped a few braincells together and rasped, "You know that's not fair."

Ashley grinned, very slowly, and ducked her head toward Penny's a little. "What's not fair?"

"Being tall like that," Penny said hoarsely.

"Well, you know I can't help being tall." Ashley suddenly got a few inches shorter as she stepped out of one of her shoes. She was abruptly so much closer, and smelled *ridiculously* good. And was still overwhelmingly tall. Her hair was all up, out of the way, but tendrils were falling around her face now that she was leaning into Penny like this. "Is that better?"

"*Better?*" Penny thought she might faint. She also thought maybe she read Ashley all wrong a couple months earlier. Maybe she had avoided looking at Penny in her bra—and not in her bra—*because* she was into her. Either that or she was the absolute most heartless woman on earth, which didn't bear thinking about. "Yes, I think…better?"

"Good. I wouldn't want to be unfair."

"Then you're going to have to stop being so beautiful, too," Penny whispered. She was fairly confident her panties were melting off. Actually, it would be great if they were, along with the rest of her clothes, because naked with Ashley sounded like the best possible place to be, but she wasn't at all sure she could manage extremely difficult things like buttons or zippers right then. God forbid she should have to navigate a bra fastener.

Ashley smiled. "You think I'm beautiful?"

"I have eyes, so, yes." That, at least, came out like someone who remembered what talking was, although Penny wasn't certain the dry sarcastic tone qualified as flirting, and she thought she should probably be trying to flirt right now.

Fortunately, Ashley threw her head back and laughed, so maybe speaking hadn't been a total disaster on Penny's part. "Thank you. I mostly think I'm gangly. You, on the other hand, are compact, petite, curvy perfection."

Penny, who was going to have to have a talk with herself later about how to flirt and also how to take a compliment, snorted dismissively. "Thanks, but I think you mean squat and bulky."

Ashley's eyebrows shot up. "I *definitely* do not."

The intensity in her voice made Penny's brain dissolve again. She should say something flirty or charming or funny. Instead she said, "Um," and swallowed again. After a moment she managed to whisper, "I'm not great at taking compliments. Except about my drumming. I'm a great drummer."

"Yeah?" Ashley pressed in, not actually quite touching Penny, but her body heat so close that she could feel it. "Got any good tricks to show me with your drumsticks?"

Penny, dizzily, said, "I could probably think of something," and the staff door banged open, destroying every fantasy she'd ever had about Ashley Torben.

"Ash!" One of Ashley's many cousins stood in the doorway, beaming and by all appearances, fully oblivious to how Ashley jerked upright and away from Penny. "Ash, okay, look, I know you were mad at me, but I've figured out a way to make it all up to you! I was just over at Miguel's, right?"

Ashley had managed to step back into her shoes already, so smoothly that even Penny hadn't noticed her do it. Her wonderful rich voice was completely controlled as she said, "Yes, Laurie, I know," in a tone that Penny suspected might not be as patient as it sounded. In fact, Penny had heard a lot of extremely exasperated parents—including her own, from time to time—use something *very* like that tone when they'd been interrupted for the ten millionth time by an aggravating child.

"So you know the Faire folks are doing the charity fundraiser for the swans? The Tundra subspecies that started nesting here a while ago? The endangered ones?"

Ashley glanced at Penny as if trying to confirm that Penny was also hearing Laurie babbling, or maybe as if she hoped Penny would understand what he was talking about. Penny, who personally wanted to kick this cousin in the shins for interrupting what had clearly been turning into an excellent moment, shrugged. Ashley exhaled, nodded once, and turned her attention back to her cousin. "No. I don't know about the charity fundraiser for the swans."

"Oh! Well, it's turned into this big thing," Laurie said brightly.

He was the youngest of Bill's brothers, Penny thought. They wouldn't miss the youngest one if she murdered him a little. Probably. There were a *lot* of other Torbens. They definitely wouldn't miss him. She was contemplating the best way to get away with murder when Laurie finished, "But there was a fire last night at the venue."

"Oh my God." Ashley's irritation fled, and so, admittedly, did Penny's. "Was anyone hurt?"

"No, not even the swans, but the venue's a loss. Miguel's panicking because they have almost two hundred people who are supposed to show up tomorrow for the fundraiser. So I said we could host it!"

The dizziness that had come over Penny a minute ago swept her again, but not in a good way this time. She happened to be exceptionally good at arranging last-minute support for large numbers of people, but two hundred unplanned guests three days before Christmas was a disaster in the making. She actually said, "You did what?" before Ashley spoke, but the pub manager managed to find her voice before Penny could lambast Laurie.

"You did *what?*"

Laurie—who was wearing his hair in incredibly intricate braids—faltered a little in his beaming smile. "I said they could have it here? We know we can handle that many people, we did it for the Sixty Pix just a few weeks ago!" He nodded at Penny like she was proof positive.

"That was October! There was no snow on the ground! We had hundreds of people *outside*! And we'd been planning an event for months so we had extra staff already lined up! And we have *two corporate holiday parties here tomorrow night, Laurie*! That's a hundred and forty people already! We can't possibly host a charity event for two hundred, or even fifty!"

"But..." Laurie stared at his cousin in dismay. "But I promised."

"Well, you're going to have to unpromise! I'm sorry, but even if I wanted to there's no way to get the staff for it, people are already leaving for their own holidays and we've had the schedule arranged for weeks! Months! And no, Laurie! What were you thinking? You can't make that kind of promise for the pub, for me!"

"But they need somewhere," Laurie said. "It's four days before Christmas. They'll never find anywhere else."

"My point exactly!"

A thought crept into Penny's mind. It was a crazy thought and she tried to ignore it, but the idea of leaving Ashley all alone to deal with the mess her cousin had made seemed unbearable, so she tentatively raised her hand. Ashley's gaze snapped toward her. "What?"

"I think...I might be able to help?"

CHAPTER 7

$\mathcal{P}$enny looked so shyly hopeful that Ashely immediately felt guilty for snapping at her. She held her breath a moment, mumbled, "Sorry for growling," and then after another holding of her breath, said, "I would appreciate any ideas."

She'd completely lost her mind already, after all. There was no way Penny had really thought she needed to return the t-shirt, which meant the Sixty Pix drummer had been looking for an excuse to come talk to her. It was apparently one thing for Ashley to approach Penny, even if she *was* her fated mate. If Penny came to her, well. It would be rude not to flirt. And Penny had looked so *cute*, admitting she would listen to Ashley read a phone book. And suggesting she could find something better for Ashley to read aloud.

Ashley really, really wanted to find out what Penny had in mind.

Which she absolutely couldn't do right now.

Thinking about how she'd leaned in to Penny, who was so tiny it was easy, was a distraction Ashley didn't need. The fact that Penny had been wide-eyed and receptive was *definitely* a distraction Ashley didn't need. At least, not while Laurie was right there, making her life even harder than it had been five minutes ago.

"We have tents," Penny said. "Venue tents, not just, like, tents for camping in. The band does, I mean. Huge ones. Wedding-sized tents."

Ashley saw where she was going with it, but said, "*Why?*" almost plaintively. "I don't think bands normally have venue tents, do they?"

"No." Penny hesitated, glancing between Ashley and Laurie, whose expression was still stricken. Ashley almost felt sorry for him. She could believe he'd been trying to be helpful. But she could also believe he really, *really* hadn't been thinking anything through, so 'almost' was as far as she went with the feeling sorry. Penny shrugged, a big loose motion that drew Ashley's attention back to her. "We've played a lot of weird venues, is the thing. In a lot of bad weather. And we have some *really* enthusiastic fans, see..."

"The Fits," Laurie said. Ashley quirked her eyebrows at him and he spread his hands. "The Sixty Pix's fans call themselves the Fits."

"Because they pitch sixty fits when they get to see us," Penny said, embarrassed. "Anyway, so we were performing at a festival a couple summers ago and the weather was incredibly bad, and the Fits decided they'd just make themselves comfortable and bring tents.

Somebody worked for a company that provided festival tents, and these ones were being retired because they'd gotten torn up a bit, so the fans rescued them, fixed them up, and after the festival asked if we wanted to keep them."

"You have somewhere to store venue tents?" Ashley asked faintly. "That must take up a lot of space."

"Myles owns a warehouse in an industrial park. *Because*," Penny said as Ashley and Laurie both boggled at her, "because he wanted somewhere to practice bass when he was a teenager, so he developed an app, some kind of game, and it did well enough that one of the big tech companies bought it, so he had money when he was like, seventeen."

"And he decided to spend his life trying to make it in a *band*?" Laurie asked incredulously. "I would have written another app and made bank."

"He did," Penny assured him. "And he's worked in the tech industry since, but yeah, in his off time, he plays bass in the band. It's not a *big* warehouse," she said, almost defensively. "But it's big enough to hold the band's gear. Including venue tents."

Ashley laughed. "Your lives aren't normal, Penny." Not that she should talk, she realized. She, after all, was the one who could turn into a bear whenever she wanted to.

"Most of the time they're very normal," Penny promised. "It's just this one aspect where it gets weird."

"Normal people haven't written game apps that get

snapped up by big companies," Laurie pointed out, then looked hopeful. "What game is it?"

"Oh, God, I don't know, I don't play phone games. It's one of those geocaching things where you run around collecting digital prizes and fighting other teams. Anyway," Penny said strenuously, "I could drive back over to Denver tonight and get the tents, if you could get the parking lot cleared to pitch them. Maybe the back lot? It's big but not as many people park there. So you could host the charity event and not risk the bookings you've already got for the main building. And I can get a lot of volunteers on short notice, although it might mean me and Gwen have to do a pick-up gig to say thanks and I should check with her first."

"What a good idea," Ashley hissed, "checking with the rest of the team before making any promises."

Laurie, who was two inches taller than she was, cowered at her tone. "I said I was sorry!"

"No you didn't!"

Her cousin froze, rolled his eyes like he was reviewing a transcript of their conversation, and winced. "I'm sorry."

"Thanks, but it doesn't help. A bunch of tents for an outdoors venue in December in Colorado doesn't seem like a great idea."

Penny, quietly but with determination, said, "Beggars can't be choosers, can they? This charity thing, they've got to know they're in a bind, right? Obviously an outdoors venue *isn't* ideal at this time of year, but they're good tents, they've got sides, so body heat and space heaters can help keep them warm-ish. But what choice do they have? Is there really any chance they'll find somewhere else on barely twenty-four hours' notice?"

"No! That's why I said we could do it!" Laurie hunched his shoulders apologetically again as Ashley gave him another glare. "Well, it is."

"Ashley!" The staff door flew open and Jon came through it, stopping abruptly to find Ashley, Penny and Laurie all crowded into the hall just a few steps beyond the door itself. He double-took at them, said, "What's going on?" and then skipped over his own question to say, "Ash, did you know the rest of your family is coming down from the mountain for the week? And that so are Uncle Richard and Aunt Pam with their crew and Uncle Dave and his kids? And that Steve and Charlee might be coming in from Virtue?"

"What? No. That's ridiculous, we just all saw each other in June at Steve's wedding. And Mom and Dad never come down from the mountains in the winter. They like to hibernate."

Penny bit back a laugh, although Ashley was completely serious. Since her youngest brother had left home a few years earlier, their parents had decided the winter months were their time to relax completely. Ashley was certain they'd slept through Christmas entirely the year before. Not that Penny could possibly know that.

Jon shrugged. "Well, Uncle Rich and Dave thought it was so great that they decided we should have another family reunion and now they're trying to get Aunt Carol and Uncle Phil to come down from wherever-the-hell-Alaska that they settled in—"

"Shkalnik," Laurie said under his breath.

Jon ignored him. "So now Mom and Dad think we should close up the pub on Christmas Eve for a family reunion."

Ashley snapped her teeth shut on her first protest, which was that they had events booked for Christmas Eve. That wasn't true, though. She'd decided that the staff deserved their holiday evening with their families, and hadn't let anybody book anything that night. There were only a couple of people scheduled to work at all, and the pub would be closing early anyway. After an incredibly long moment of trying to think of a way out of it, her shoulders slumped. "It's their pub. I guess I can't really say no."

Penny was counting on her fingers. "Pete, Richard, Dave, Phil, and…your dad, Ashley? There are five Elder Torben brothers?"

"Phil is Aunt Carol's husband. She's the Torben. Her and Aunt Rachel are the two girls, and then there's, yeah. Four brothers. And I only have a brother and a sister, but everybody else has at least four kids."

Penny went back to counting on her fingers. "So you have twenty-one cousins?"

Ashley sighed. "Twenty-three, actually."

"But that's just on the Torben side," Laurie said. "Mom's got three sisters and they've all got two or three kids. Except Aunt Lily. She's just got Ollie, and moved to Australia."

"You have *thirty* cousins?"

And that, Ashley thought, was why she'd wanted to get to know Penny without the madness of her huge family around. Huge, both in number and in actual size: there were several cousins shorter than she was, but none of them was less than five ten. Penny, at barely over five feet, would actually disappear into the crowd. She said, "Lily and Mom's other sisters aren't coming, are they?"

"I don't think Aunt Lily is ever leaving Australia again," Jon said. "She moved there to get away from all of us, and since Ollie found his maaaaarriage partner at Steve's wedding she doesn't have to fly back to the States for any of that kind of thing."

Ashley bugged her eyes at him, and he bugged his back. Shifters weren't usually so careless about mentioning fated mates in front of true humans, but there weren't usually three shifters and only one human hanging around, either. When there was, the one human was often someone's mate.

Which, of course, Penny was. Ashley just hadn't told her that yet. Ashley hadn't told her anything, because she was a big wobbly coward, and now poor Penny was going to be overwhelmed with Torbens and run away to be a rock star without ever wanting to see Ashley again.

Ashley's bear gazed at her patiently until she stopped running in mental circles like that and sighed.

Okay, fine, but really, nobody should be subjected to forty or fifty Torbens before a first date!

Then you should take your mate on a first date, the bear said calmly.

"I don't have time!" The words burst out, aloud. Both her cousins grimaced at her, clearly understanding she'd been arguing with her bear and had slipped up, but Penny, who had no idea what was going on, patted Ashley's arm sympathetically.

"You're right, you really don't. It'd be bad enough getting a charity event dumped on you—"

Jon's eyes widened. "What? Oh, the swans thing? I heard about the fire at their venue. We're hosting it? That's great! Thanks, Ash! The Faire folk are going to be really relieved, they've been setting up for this for months. They've even got a celebrity guest. Do you know, uh, oh, what's her name." He dug his phone out, saying, "The professional wrestler with All-Arena Entertainment? Maggie somebody. Ross!" he said as his phone gave him the information he was looking for. "Apparently she's really into swan conservationism, who knew? I didn't even know they were endangered anywhere. Anyway, that's really great, Ash, you're gonna be the hero of the hour!"

Ashley very carefully didn't look at Laurie, who was beaming hopefully at her and wasn't even trying to take credit for thinking of having the pub host the suddenly-unhoused benefit event. Probably wise, because she would have tried flushing him down a toilet, or something. "I guess."

Penny, whose sympathy had gotten entirely run over by Jon's enthusiasm, gave Ashley another pat on the arm. Her hand was small and warm, and Ashley had the impulse to take it and kiss her knuckles, but that would have opened her up for so much teasing from her cousins, and she couldn't explain about the mate bond right then, with Penny standing right there. "Okay," she said to Penny, stiffly. "I guess I'm going to have to take you up on the offer for those tents, but only if you're really, really sure. It's a long drive and it's already getting late."

"It's fine, really." Penny smiled up at her, a bright generous expression. "The truth is I'm great in an emergency, and I was feeling weird and awkward about crashing your family's Christmas already, so if I can help then that'll make me less weird about it all."

"Please don't ever feel awkward," Ashley said quickly. "You have no idea how nice it is to have you here. Everything else aside, there are so freaking many guy cousins. Any extra women make it better, and you're really great."

"Oh." Penny beamed. "You're great too. Look, it's already seven so I'll probably drive to Denver, go to sleep, and get the tents early in the morning and drive back. Will that be okay?"

"It will be," Laurie blurted. "It'll be perfect. It's amazing. Thank you so much. Ashley, I'll be here first thing in the morning to clear the lot, okay? I promise I won't make it any more work for you than it absolutely has to be."

Jon, obviously sensing he'd missed some things, cautiously said, "And I'll tell everybody the pub's closing at five on Christmas Eve, and do all the setup for the family reunion?"

Ashley flung her hands upward. "Okay, fine! You've got it all under control! That's great! Go...go do the thing!" She felt far more exasperated than she should, given that her cousins were doing literally what she'd asked them to, which was pick up the slack. But she *hadn't* asked them to also add a ton of work to her schedule, either. Although she guessed a last-minute family reunion was her aunt and uncle's fault, not her cousins'.

Either way, they scattered like they felt like they were lucky to escape with their lives, and Ashley was left with Penny smiling up at her again. "If the charity's other venue was planning a big event, they've probably got a lot of the staff lined up already. If you can check about that and then text me whatever you find out, I'll get volunteers for—oh, I better talk to Gwen. Come with me?" She tilted toward the door, smiling hopefully, and Ashley, enthralled, walked after her in a daze.

CHAPTER 8

"It'll be okay," Penny promised over her shoulder to Ashley, who was following her with a slightly stunned expression. "The charity event and the family reunion both getting dumped on you is a lot. Are you okay?"

"I have no idea," Ashley admitted. "I could kill Laurie, but I probably can't kill my entire extended family."

"I mean, it'd have to be a whole Jonestown kind of thing," Penny agreed. "There are too many of them to knock off one at a time. Oh good, there's Gwen, right where I left her. Well, she wasn't in Bill's lap when I left them, but..." Her bandmate and her boyfriend were in one of the pub's booths, and if Gwen wasn't actually *quite* in Bill's lap, it was pretty close. "Okay, you two, cut it out, stop being gross, we have an emergency." She slid into the other half of the booth, gesturing for

Ashley to join her, and felt a little thrill of delight as Ashley's arm brushed hers when they sat down.

That was full-on goofy crush material, being excited over little touches like that, and she had more important things to think about right then. Gwen turned worried attention to them, although her worry faded as Penny outlined the situation. "Oh. That kind of emergency. I thought you meant an *emergency*-emergency. Yeah, of course, we can do a pick-up gig or something if we need to call out the Fits for their volunteer services. I can get Ripley to come play second guitar if we want it to be more than just us. Do you need company driving back to Denver?"

Penny, watching Bill's face fall even though he tried to hide it, smiled at her lead singer. "Nah, G, you just got back to this dude. I'm not gonna steal you away from him tonight. There's usually some dudes at the warehouse district who will help a lil' tiny lady like myself move heavy stuff, and I can do any Fits recruiting on the drive, if I need to."

"Is that safe?" Ashley asked worriedly. "Texting and driving?"

"I've got a good voice to text thing set up," Penny promised. "Oh, but let me give you my number so you can text about how many volunteers we might need."

She took Ashley's phone, putting her number in as Gwen, dryly, said, "Or I could wrangle the Fits, if we need them. I'll be right here and able to get the word from the horse's mouth." She nodded at Ashley.

Bill muttered, "Bear's mouth," which made Gwen

laugh and, from the sudden sharp movement, made Ashley kick him under the table. He looked credibly injured, although he was about six and a half feet tall and Penny wasn't sure anything less than a bulldozer hitting him in the shins could hurt him.

"Well, now you've got my number anyway," she said, giving Ashley's phone back. "If it turns out everybody's a total idiot, you can call me and we'll run away to Peru together."

"Do we have to wait for everybody to prove they're idiots, or could we just make a break for it?" Ashley scooted out of the booth when Penny, laughing, nudged her.

"You could just leave it all up to your cousins while we ran," she suggested. "But if we're gonna, you should tell me now so I don't have to drive to Denver first."

"You'd have to drive to Denver anyway," Gwen pointed out. "You can't get a flight to Peru from Renaissance."

"Then I wouldn't have to wait for Ashley to drive there, too! We could just go together!"

"I can't," Ashley said regretfully. "I can't even just drive with you tonight. We're supposed to be crazy busy for the rest of the night."

"Well, next time," Penny said, and meant it. "I'll be back by eleven tomorrow morning, maybe a bit earlier. Don't do anything I wouldn't do," she said to the three of them in general, and headed out to Denver with Ashley Torben's warm voice and the memory of her leaning presence fresh in her mind. It kept her company on the whole long drive.

DRIVING three hours back and forth to Denver in a day was one thing, Penny decided the next morning as she pulled back into the Thunder Bear Pub parking lot. But she and Gwen had driven *from* Denver the previous afternoon, too, so she'd spent about ten out of the past twenty-four hours in a car, and that was a bit much. Her butt was numb. Her toes were cold. She'd slept well the previous night, but she also wanted a long nap and a massage. Alternately, anything to get the blood flowing would be good.

Just as she parked, just as she had that thought, Ashley Torben walked out of the pub, talking on her phone. Penny's heart thumped and she gave a breathy little laugh. Yeah, that would get the blood flowing for sure. She'd never seen Ashley dressed up: the pub manager wore jeans and a bulky sweater right now, one that looked like it had maybe been hand-knit. Her hair was in a ponytail again, a fluffy dark golden mass that haloed around her head. She spoke with anima-tion, her free hand waving in the air and her expres-sion going irritated and amused by the moment. She hung up as Penny got out of the van, said something to the sky, then squinted toward Penny before a wide smile split her face and she called, "You're back! Was the drive okay?"

"Yup, but I need to do about a hundred squats because my ass is like a wood block right now. Laurie—Laurie? Was it Laurie who said he'd clean up the parking lot? He's done a good job." When Penny had left the night before, there'd been snow packed to ice all over the parking lot, and small banks of snow everywhere. Now it was scraped down to the asphalt, with—"Are those space heaters?"

There were about twenty of them, all remarkably large and all spaced evenly around the parking lot, with long extension cords running back to the pub. Ashley, wryly exasperated, said, "They are. He apparently borrowed them from Faire folk who use them in the spring and fall when the weather starts to get cold. His logic was that if he aimed them at the parking lot, any ice melt would dry up instead of re-freezing. I'm pretty sure it's a terrible waste of electricity, but it's also working, and since I don't want to be liable if anybody slips on ice tonight, I don't have a better idea."

"They'll be perfect for keeping the tents warm, too. How are you holding up with the unexpected additions to the schedule?" Penny hauled the back of the van open and gestured inside as Ashley came around to look. The guys at the warehouse had helped her load hundreds of square feet worth of festival tents into the van, and now she had every intention of letting Ashley's large cousins do all the heavy lifting of unloading it. "Think this will do?"

"I have no idea," Ashley said, mystified. "I've never seen festival tents lying down before."

"Really." Penny grinned. "I'll have to lie down in one with you."

A blush ran up Ashley's jaw and she cast Penny a startled glance. Penny, grinning even more widely, said, "Sorry. Sorry? We are doing the flirting thing, aren't we? Or was that leaning over me last night thing just messing with me?"

"No," Ashley said, still obviously startled. "No, I wasn't messing with you. Not if you meant it about liking my voice."

"Oh, I meant it."

A little smile crept over the tall woman's mouth. "So, yes. Yes, we're doing the flirting thing."

"That's the best news I've heard in at least a month, and let me tell you, this past month has had a lot of good news." Penny let herself lean toward Ashley a little, feeling the other woman's warmth, then gave a huge sigh. "Now that we've got the flirting thing established, I'm afraid we might have to put it aside until we've got this whole event of yours—"

"Not mine!" Ashley objected strenuously, which made Penny laugh.

"Yeah, true, not yours. Okay, until we've got this whole event of Laurie's dealt with. It's actually going to go fine, you know that, right?" She glanced up—so very far up—at Ashley's slightly tense expression, and bumped her hip against hers. "Honestly, it's going to be fine. The other event venue people have most of the staff they need lined up, you said in text last night that you were able to call a few of your own people in for overtime, and the Fits will show up to work crowd control and keep parking and accessibility under control. It's going to be fine."

"You know, Gwen did this to Bill, too. Swept in and fixed everything when it was going to hell for him."

"Please." Penny sniffed. "I did a *ton* of that fixing."

Ashley smiled again, tentatively. "Yeah. What's that about? Is it the Sixty Pix's secret super power? You can turn any disaster into a hit concert? Hey!" Her voice lifted suddenly and she waved some of her cousins down. "Come be useful! This van needs unloading!"

One of them—a dude, but most of them seemed to be—waved from the other side of the parking lot, indicating he'd heard and they'd be there in a minute. Ashley turned to lean against the inside floor of the van a little and mumbled, "Sorry, I interrupted whatever you were going to say."

"By hailing strong men to do heavy lifting instead of me doing it, so I approve." Penny leaned against the van with her. "We've played so many crazy venues over the past ten years or so that we've just gotten really, really good at reacting on the fly, I think. Things are always going wrong and it's great if there's a team in place to fix it, but it's not like we've been selling out stadium tours."

"Yet," Ashley said warmly.

To her surprise, Penny felt her face heat up. She hunched her shoulders and smiled at the cold ground. "Yet. I hope. But the point is a big professional venue is going to have a sound team, a tech team, in place to make everything work smoothly. We haven't had that kind of support, so we've gotten really good at figuring it out and making it happen on our own. If we start getting real support we'll probably lose our minds and be horrible divas who shout at people for doing the work around us wrong because we're so used to doing it ourselves."

"I doubt that. It's probably more likely you'll get in the way because you want to help and you'll be so nice about it people will feel bad about telling you no."

Penny pursed her lips. "That actually sounds really likely, yeah. I guess we'll just have to get so big and famous we can't possibly be available to help because we'll get mugged if we're out laying speaker wires or something."

Ashley laughed and tried twice to find a response to that before she could really talk. "On one hand, that sounds great for you, but on the other, people wanting to mug you is bad!"

"Maybe I'll employ a tall Amazonian bodyguard. It's working pretty well for Gwen."

"Bill isn't Amazonian," Ashley pointed out with amusement.

"No, he's…well, whatever the male equivalent of Amazonian is, but you know what I mean. How *are* you doing with all the chaos?" Penny asked again. Ashley's cousins were collecting at the other side of the parking lot, with Laurie, whose hair was still in the intricate braids, now gesturing and giving orders. The group of large men finally nodded and headed toward the van, so Penny stood up, and Ashley moved away with her.

"I'm less freaked out than I was last night," Ashley admitted. "You're pretty reassuring, and having these tents available makes all the difference."

"Me. Reassuring." Penny laughed. "I think large solid presences are reassuring. I probably qualify as solid, but not large. Here, guys." She went forward again to explain how the tents went together, not because it was difficult, but because it was faster to show them than to let them figure it out. Within a few minutes, there were half-erected tent poles with fabric vinyl walls—or something, Penny didn't actually know what the tent material itself was—flopping between them.

"We got this," Laurie announced to Ashley. "We'll get them set up and I'll come in to find you and get your okay on the layout and everything, okay?"

"You should get my okay on the layout before you have it set up, or you might have to move everything," Ashley protested.

Penny put her hand on Ashley's arm. "There are an incredibly limited number of ways they can put them up, so they're not going to have to move anything. In the meantime, it's eleven in the morning and I, for one, haven't eaten anything except a bad cup of coffee and a worse doughnut from a gas station just outside of Denver. So unless you're actually supposed to be at work right now, I think instead of worrying about how they lay the whole thing out, you should probably take me over to that diner down the street and feed me."

Ashley blinked at her. "I haven't eaten either…"

"I didn't think so." Penny, feeling smug at guessing right, slid her arm through Ashley's. "So. Breakfast, and then we'll come back and admire all the heavy lifting your big strong handsome cousins have done."

Ashley, bemused, said, "Okay," and Penny led her off toward the diner.

CHAPTER 9

$\mathcal{A}$shley was beginning to think Penny got her own way a lot. Otherwise she, Ashley, would not be walking Penny to the diner. Instead she would be standing around the parking lot worrying and fussing and, she reluctantly concluded, possibly, just *possibly*, being in the way. They were at a table and warming up in the cozy diner before she said, "How did you do that?" in a tone that sounded mystified even to her own ears.

Penny set the menu aside and grinned across the table at her. "I think you have a lot in common with your cousin Bill. Very responsible, maybe a little uptight about making sure things get done because you don't quite trust anybody else to do it, probably with good reason. But not everything needs your immediate and constant supervision. I speak from the experience of having learned this the hard way myself. So I appealed—"

Despite herself, Ashley laughed. "To my better nature?"

"Oh, God, no. 'Never appeal to a man's better nature. He may not have one. Invoking his self-interest gives you more leverage.' Although I'm constantly amazed at how many people actually vote against their own self-interests, but never mind that. That's a long way of saying I figured you were hungry and that suggesting food would outweigh your sense of responsibility for keeping an eye on a bunch of grown men who have been given the equivalent of a giant Lego set to put together."

"You're just very confident, aren't you?" Ashley sat back in the booth, staring at Penny in admiration. The Sixty Pix drummer was small and compact, but then, Ashley thought, so were firecrackers, and they made a hell of a sound. "Was that a quote, the thing about better natures? It sounded like one."

"Yeah, an old science fiction writer said it. Robert Heinlein. And look, yeah, I hit things really hard for a living—well, not a living, but for a hobby—well, not a hobby, I do get paid for it—anyway, the point is, I'm really *short* and the best way to get people to take me seriously is to not only be brazenly confident about everything, but also *right* about everything, like, all the time."

Ashley gave a startled laugh. "And are you?"

Penny offered a positively rakish grin. "Often enough, yeah. Besides, we're both going to be increasingly busy as today goes on, I think, so if we're doing the flirting thing I thought I should get you alone to do that for a little while. So tell me about Ashley Torben."

The rakish grin made Ashley's heart flutter, but the much softer smile that followed Penny's last few words made her insides positively melt. "You've got a very direct way of flirting."

"It's Gwen's fault. I learned from her. Is it working?"

Part of Ashley wanted to explain it wouldn't matter if Penny didn't flirt at all. That Ashley would happily follow her around adoringly just to get the time of day, never mind a series of devastating smiles and direct, laughing comments. That she knew in her soul that the confident redheaded drummer was everything that would make her happy in life.

Of course, all that also required her explaining that she could turn into a bear and that her certainty that they belonged together was born out of a magic that had served shifters well over the millennia. That didn't seem like the right conversation to have in a diner, so Ashley only ducked her head and murmured, "Yeah, I think it is."

"Amazing. What's good here?" Penny waved a hand, indicating the diner, and Ashley took a moment to look around like it was a place new to her.

It was *not* an elegant space, or even a charmingly retro one. Larry's Diner had been in Renaissance as long as anybody could remember, and the decor hadn't really been updated since the seventies. Inexpensive brown beadboard panelling covered the lower half of the walls, with scarring where olive green vinyl booths had come loose and gotten scraped against them. More than one of those booth seats had been repaired with duct tape. The tables were metal-based, with faintly yellowed laminate tops that sported paper placemats that doubled as the menus. The lighting was dim, especially in winter when the nights closed in early, although for the moment it was as bright as it got, with sunlight bouncing off the snow outside and reflecting through the windows. The whole place looked like a hole in the wall. It *was* a hole in the wall.

Ashley looked back at Penny and smiled. "Everything. Literally everything is good here. Not just good. Homemade levels of good. I have a real weakness for the chicken-fried steak and eggs, personally, but you can't go wrong with anything on the menu."

"You know what, Bill said the same thing when he brought us here for dinner before our first gig at the pub, and the hot wings I got were fantastic, but I thought maybe I'd lucked out. Two locals telling me the same thing, though. Now I'm starting to trust it, and also starting to understand why a place that looks like the last half of last century forgot about it is still open and doing good business."

"It does look like that, doesn't it? I'm used to it, but yeah. Whatever you order will be good." A waiter came by as Ashley finished speaking, and although the guy, in his fifties, looked as worn out and used up as the diner itself did, he smiled.

"That's what we like to hear. We doing breakfast or lunch, ladies?"

Penny said, "Yes," and ordered the Big Blue, which involved buttermilk pancakes with blueberries, blueberry yogurt, hash browns, eggs, bacon, and a blueberry 'smoothie' that Ashley knew was basically a milkshake. When the meal arrived a few minutes later, Penny stared at the hash browns in dismay. "They're blue."

Ashley, who had been waiting for that, grinned. "You did order a breakfast called 'Big Blue.'"

"But the potatoes are blue!"

"They're some kind of Peruvian potato," Ashley said, still grinning. "Aren't they cool?"

"They're *blue*!" Penny took an incredibly cautious bite and managed to look even more dismayed. "And they taste exactly like potatoes. They're delicious. Okay, somebody call the chef, this is amazing. What the heck!" She pointed her fork at Ashley. "Are you using mysterious foods to distract me from asking you to tell me about yourself? It's not working, if you are."

"I don't know that there's all that much to tell," Ashley protested. "I grew up in Renaissance, or up in the mountains just above it, have nine thousand cousins and a business degree, and I run a pub."

And you turn into a bear, her bear concluded.

Yes, but I can't say that over brunch!

Why not? The bear sounded affronted. *She's your mate. She'll believe you.*

She really won't, Ashley promised. *It's too weird.* "So that's boring me," she said, to drown out the bear. "What about you?"

"I grew up in Denver, decided I wanted to be Animal when I was like five years old, pestered my parents into buying me a drum kit, and am now living the dream as the drummer for the Sixty Pix. Animal," she repeated when Ashley blinked at her in confusion. "From the Muppets."

Ashley laughed out loud, taken completely by surprise. "Oh. That's wonderful. Really?"

"Really. All that energy and noise. It was great. I also have a day job as a housecleaner," Penny added. "Because it turns out you can't really bank on being a rock star. No, really," she said to Ashley's new round of surprise. "I'm an independent contractor, so I can make my own hours, which means not scheduling myself when we've got a gig. And I'm really good at it. I took a course in crime scene cleanup."

Ashley stopped with a forkful of food halfway to her mouth. "Are you kidding?"

"I am not kidding. I decided I didn't want to do actual crime scene cleanup because trauma, but it was really interesting and there's basically nothing I can't clean now."

"You are a *much* more interesting person than I am," Ashley said aloud, and, to her bear, *I know fate is never wrong but there's no way she'll want to stay with someone like me. I'm completely ordinary.*

"Eh." Penny shrugged. "Different. I can clean a crime scene and bang a drum. I could not, however, run a pub or get a business degree."

"That seems unlikely!"

Penny smiled. "I'm not great at sitting down and studying unless I can either make a lot of noise while I'm doing it, or it's something new and fascinating with basically every turn of the page."

Ashley tilted her head, cautiously curious. "ADHD? You don't have to answer, obviously, I'm just being nosy."

Penny lifted two fingers close together. "Lil' bit, yeah. I'm pretty focused as long as I remember my meds, but I tell you what, expecting people who struggle with routine to take two pills a day to keep their heads on straight is a big ask. But I think it's part of why I'm great in an emergency. It's a whole new situation with constant challenges that is resolved in a relatively short period of time! I'm great at that! But I get bored and lose interest if it turns into an ongoing series of basically repetitive challenges."

"Like running a pub."

The redhead touched a fingertip to her nose. "Exactly. So, see? Different, that's all, not more or less interesting. Besides, I think you are interesting. Wrangling all those cousins, running that pub, throwing beers on women to get their attention…"

Ashley laughed and hid her face in her hands. "Not my usual approach."

"Worked though, didn't it? Although I thought you weren't interested," Penny said. "You wouldn't even look at me."

"Only because you were so knee-meltingly hot I thought I would actually drool on you if I did," Ashley said into her hands. "I mean, come on, you were half naked in the bathroom and you've got the most *incredible*...biceps...." That was true, if not exactly the body part Ashley had been trying not to look at.

Penny didn't respond, and after a moment Ashley looked up to find the other woman beaming shyly at her. "People don't usually call me hot," she said. "Cute, yes, but not hot. Cute is the curse of the short woman."

"I'm sorry, but you are cute," Ashley said. "Button nose and everything. But also hot. I mean. Look at you." She made a small helpless gesture. "You're *stacked*. Whereas I'm tall and sort of twiggy."

Penny's eyebrows rose so high they were in danger of getting lost in her hairline. "First, Twiggy is a literal fashion icon. Second, I don't think you're seeing the same person I am when I look at you. Not to come on too strong, but I would walk across a bed of molten lava for an ounce of your elegance."

"I poured a beer on you."

A startled laugh burst from Penny's chest and she pushed the rest of her food away, having made quite a dent as they'd chatted. "Even the elegant are clumsy sometimes. But seriously, look, my life is nuts and I know that, and I don't know if brunch as a distraction to keep you from micromanaging counts as a date, but if you'd be interested I'd really like to take you out on a *real* date sometime this week? Next week? We're in town through the end of the year."

"I do not micromanage!" Ashley hesitated. "I don't think I micromanage."

"You probably don't, actually. Sorry, I didn't mean to hit a sore spot there." Penny bit her lower lip, which had the perhaps-unfortunate effect of making her look even cuter. She had large, dark brown eyes beneath her shaggy red haircut, and her uncertainty gave her a pretty terrific puppy-dog look just then. "Is that a nice way of letting me down? By avoiding the question?"

"No! No, I'd love to go out with you on a real date. If this isn't one. Is this one?"

Penny smiled. "No. Because I can definitely do better than this for a first date. I mean, I hear there's this big gala charity event happening at the Thunder Bear Brewpub tonight, and I'd totally take you to that, but it's so last-minute I'm afraid you're already working."

"Well, *I* hear the lead singer and drummer from the Sixty Pix might show up to that event, so you probably wouldn't want to be stuck with me tonight anyway, but maybe..." Ashley tried to think ahead and ended up groaning. "God, maybe tonight is actually best. I'm working the next two nights and then my insane family has decided to have a last-minute reunion and there's no way I'm introducing you to seven million Torbens on a first date. It'd be like running you through the gauntlet."

"Well." Penny leaned forward, moved Ashley's plate out of the way, and put her hand down, palm up, as an invitation. "Let's say we called this a first date, and the thing tonight a second date. Then you could spare me the gauntlet until the *third* date, and I'm sure that would be totally fine, right?"

"I'm not sure you really appreciate how *many* of us there are."

"I've met about a dozen of you already," Penny said gamely. "Give me a chance."

Ashley, knowing she sounded way too soppy, murmured, "There's nothing I'd rather do," and put her hand into Penny's.

olding hands wasn't supposed to actually make little electric shocks run through her. Penny was fairly sure of that. But she swore that she felt a *zing* as Ashley folded her hand into Penny's, and that delicious feeling kept zipping through her, a warm memory, for the rest of the afternoon.

It had to, because once they left the diner, both women were pulled opposite directions and into different kinds of chaos. Penny caught glimpses of Ashley now and then when the pub manager came out to check up on the raising of the barn, or at least, of the event tents. God, she was lovely. A commanding presence. Just beautiful. And willing to try giving Penny Partridge, a shrimp from Denver, a chance at dating her.

Penny was insanely lucky already, what with the Sixty Pix going viral and the sudden leap in their popularity, but even that barely held a candle to the idea of taking Ashley on a real date. She didn't know how she would manage to make that evening, with both of them having their own schedules, something special, but she was determined to try. And the first, most critical thing, was to grab Ashley's cousin Laurie, who had started the whole event mess, and say, "This thing tonight, is it a dress-up thing? Do we get to be fancy?"

"It's not formal," Laurie said cautiously. "Even if it had been gonna be, that was before it was being held in a parking lot. But it wasn't gonna be anyway. There'll be a lot of people in garb, though, because it's sponsored by the local Renaissance Faire people."

"Right." Penny stared at him. He was tall and lighter blonde than his brothers, but otherwise looked exactly like the rest of them, as far as she was concerned. "What's 'garb?'"

Laurie blinked, then laughed. "Renaissance-era-style clothes. Or fairy court stuff, even. Kind of fantasy things? Medieval stuff? That kind of thing."

"Right." Penny nodded, still squinting up at him. "Does Ashley have anything like that?"

"Oh, God, yeah. She used to do the faires with us and she had some great stuff. She had this terrific elfin costume and used to do her hair in braids." He gestured at his own hair in its intricate thin braids. "I stopped doing the elf stuff after she quit but I'm getting back into it for next year. It's gotten really popular again."

"Right," Penny said a third time. "Can you get her costume? Her elf costume? And get her to do her hair?"

Laurie's eyebrows rose. "There is zero chance my

cousin is going to sit down and do her hair when she's got all this going on."

"Tell her it's for a date." Penny marched off, thinking, as Laurie yelled, "A date with who?"

She didn't have 'garb' or anything that could even pretend to pass as elf-y, but this was a town called Renaissance that held a huge Renaissance Faire every year. There had to be *somewhere* she could rent a costume. And maybe get her hair done. "Gwen!"

Her bandmate was helping set up a small stage at the back of one of the tents, and stood up in a flurry of wires and wrenches. "Yeah?"

"Can Bill recommend a Renaissance garb store around here?"

"Probably, just a second." Gwen put a wrench in one pocket and took her phone out of another, starting to text and then making a face before actually *calling* Bill with it. Penny watched in vague horror as she did that, and was stunned when he apparently answered. Either that or Gwen had lost her mind and was talking to nobody, but since she hung up and said, "There are five of them. One's really high-end, three are in it to sell to tourists, and one is the store most of the locals use. He'll text you the addresses, but the nice one is up the road from the Harlequin music club, if that helps."

"Oh, yeah, it does. I'll go there and if they don't have what I'm looking for I'll try the one the locals use. Thanks!" She drove off in the van, grateful that Renaissance had sensible streets that went in order, and found her way to the first of the costume shops. It was clear, just from the window display, that it was both out of her price range and intended for people shaped like six-foot-tall slender Ashley, not like short and stubby Penny. She went in anyway, and to her delight found that the proprietor was barely taller than she was, and definitely not svelte by anyone's definition.

"This is ridiculously beautiful stuff," Penny said wistfully as she drifted through the store. The owner was at a sewing machine, nominally putting together something in shimmering dark blue fabric with stars and moons embroidered in delicate gold, although she was mostly smiling and watching Penny as she examined the gowns. Some looked like actual leaves had been sewn together in dozens of gold and red shades, or were the bright welcoming colors of spring. There were lightweight cloaks that glimmered like sunlight on water, and fanciful concoctions that supported wings or sweeping shoulders or curving threads of wire that caught the light like magic dust was floating around the dress. "I don't suppose you rent any of these things…"

The owner, who wore a name tag that said *Karina*, smiled. "Not usually, but it's the middle of winter, so I'm less likely to be selling much. We can probably arrange something."

Penny, glancing outside, said, "I'm surprised you're even open at this time of year, now that you've mentioned it."

"Well, this is where my sewing machines are." Karina grinned. "Since I'm here to sew anyway, it's no skin off my back to keep the door unlocked and have people wander in. Mostly it's quiet, though. Starts picking up in March and then there's usually an influx of people who decide to get married at the faire and want something special for it. What colors do you like?"

"Anything that clashes with my hair," Penny suggested.

"Purple and orange it is," Karina agreed.

An hour later Penny had a dress rented, and an appointment with somebody who could apparently do something appealing with her choppy short hair. It took much, much longer to deal with her hair than she anticipated, to the point that she started sending Gwen in-progress pictures along with notes that said *No wonder I blow it dry without looking and call it good. How do people stand actually doing their hair every day? Or their makeup?!*

Gwen, whose own makeup was on point in a way Penny could only envy, sent back laughing emojis. *The secret to the makeup is a bold red lipstick and then nobody notices anything else.*

You lie, Penny wrote, and then had to put the phone down while the hairdresser wrangled her head around. She had to admit the end result was awfully satisfying, though, and only took a little convincing to let them send her next door to a place that would do her makeup, too.

Of course, she was setting Ashley up for terrible disappointment, by getting all gussied up like this.

Neither housecleaning nor drumming required dressing nicely, and Penny couldn't currently remember the last time she'd really dressed up. Even the TV interviews over the past month had mostly been jeans-and-t-shirts sorts of affairs, although there had been a couple fancy enough to justify a cute dress or two. But that was several steps below 'trying to impress a girl at a gala,' even if it was a gala held in a parking lot under festival tents and kept warm with giant space heaters.

It was dark by the time she got back to the pub—the sun set just before five at this time of year—but the event tents were all set up and looked terrific. Penny went to find Gwen to make sure they would be ready to play later that evening. They were, but mostly, her bandmate took one look at her, said, "Oh my God, you look *fabulous*. I've got to up my game! See you in a couple of hours," and ran off to get ready.

That, Penny thought, was a good sign. Maybe Ashley would be equally impressed.

She pulled the cloak she'd rented tighter around her shoulders and went through the tents, looking at everything that had been set up. There was a Christmas tree with a bunch of fake birds in it, and shining rings to brighten it up, mistletoe strung everywhere, little LED tree lights in multiple rows giving the whole space a surprisingly soft warm glow, and a startling number of people already there. From their outfits, some of them were definitely staff, but a lot were in what Penny now recognized as 'garb,' which did range from some very real-looking medieval-y stuff to fairy outfits even more fanciful than her own.

An unexpected number were musicians. Penny eyed the stage she and Gwen had helped set up. It was meant to hold quite a few people, but she didn't think it would manage a dozen or so musicians with lutes and drums and flutes and whatever else people were carrying. Especially not with *her* drum set already up there.

Well, it wasn't her problem. She and Gwen would have the stage to themselves at the end of the evening. If everybody else was cramming up their on their own earlier than that, then they could deal with it. There were dancers, too, people working out some kind of stage performance that they'd probably had rehearsed just fine before they ended up in a tent with poles in their way. Penny was reasonably confident they'd figure it out, and thought that if there was this much entertainment here already, it might turn out to be a pretty great evening.

She took a moment to look into the pub, hoping to find Ashley, but backed out again slowly. The holiday parties Ashley had mentioned were in full swing, with one rowdy group in the eighty-person event hall and another one crowded into the stage end of the pub. Not that the stage was set up now, but it had been down next to the beer garden's main entrance, when the Sixty Pix had played there in October. Now there was a party that spilled out into the beer garden, and a considerable number of other patrons stuffed into the pub as well.

Penny decided that Ashley didn't need her as a distraction, and that it was very unlikely the pub manager would have time to dress up. "In which case," she said to herself as she retreated to her van, where it was warm and quiet, "I hope she doesn't think you're totally ridiculous for dressing up yourself, Pen."

Ashley might not. By the time the charity event doors were actually open at seven, Penny herself thought she was ridiculous. She liked wearing cute summer dresses when she wasn't working, but she didn't wear fairy costumes, and she didn't wear this much makeup, and she didn't get her hair done, like, *ever*. Both housecleaning and drumming were sweaty jobs. Doing more than raking some mousse or spritzing hairspray through her hair was as *done* as it ever got. She looked stupid, felt stupid, and worst of all, was so dolled up she would have to go back to her hotel to shower and start all over again to get out of this get-up, and she didn't have time.

Instead, she sat in the front seat of her van, slumped down and seriously considering never getting out of it again. If she sat there long enough she could freeze to death, and that would be better than embarrassing herself by overdressing for a maybe-not-even-a-real-date with Ashley Torben.

Sadly for her, long before she was in any actual danger of freezing to death—particularly since she had the heater on—Gwen pounded on the van window. "What are you doing in there!" she yelled through it.

"The party is over there! Maggie Ross is here! You gotta meet her!"

Penny, somewhat sullenly, rolled the window down. "Really? She's here already? I thought somebody like her would show up really late, stay for five minutes, and disappear again."

"She's in there telling everybody that if they behave themselves she might get her husband to bring in the biggest swan anybody's ever seen. More importantly, she's already gotten him to cut a five quintillion dollar check for the charity fundraiser, so everybody's really in a partying mood now. C'mon!" Gwen jigged impatiently. She'd come back to the party in a black leather dress that wasn't even vaguely Renaissance-y, but was very, very rock star, and her signature wine-colored lipstick lit up her smile like a beacon. "C'mooooon!"

"Okay, okay, fine." Penny killed the engine and crawled out of the van, letting Gwen help her because there were a ridiculous number of layers to her skirt. "I feel stupid. Who is Maggie Ross married to?"

"You look incredible. Her husband is the owner of All-Arena Entertainment. He's *the* professional wrestling guy."

"Oh. Oh, that Conroy Loyal guy or whatever? Yeah, I've heard of him. I didn't know she'd married him. He better *worship* her, man."

"Conri Lyell, yeah. And judging from the size of the check he wrote, he absolutely does. C'mooooon." Gwen tugged Penny's elbow, dragging her toward the charity gala, which, Penny had to admit, *sounded* like a great party. She could hear the flautists somewhere in the crowd, playing Christmas carols with a couple of reasonably quiet drummers supporting them. There was an incredibly tall blond woman in the crowd, but it wasn't Ashley, and Penny's heart dropped with disappointment.

"Have you seen Ashley?"

"No, not yet—hey, wait!" Gwen made sounds of protest as Penny peeled off, heading toward the pub, then sighed and yelled, "Well, don't forget to come back to the party!" after her.

"I won't!" Penny just wanted to make sure Ashley would be there. Celebrity pro wrestlers were cool, but not the person Penny was interested in seeing. Even if Ash hadn't had the chance to dress up, maybe they could still make it a date.

Another tall blond came out of the pub, her hair swept up in intricate braids that put Laurie's to shame, wearing a high-collared green gown so elegant that Penny didn't recognize her as Ashley for a few seconds. She looked *regal*, like there should be an emerald crown in her hair. The gown was lined in thin strands of silver, making her look even taller and more slender than she was, and Penny couldn't help a despairing laugh. She was a hobbit who had fallen for an elf. A small, roundish, brightly-colored hobbit. It was impossible.

CHAPTER 11

There were hundreds of people at the charity event already, and somehow, through all the noise and the irregular lighting and crowds, Ashley still heard Penny's laugh through it all. She turned that direction, looking for the petite redhead, and found her in the first glance.

Her mate looked a little confused and overwhelmed and uncertain. All of those things, and also *incredibly* beautiful. A smile crashed across Ashley's face and she pushed through the crowd, going the wrong way until she broke through at Penny's side and grabbed her hands, beaming at her. "Oh my God, look at you! Where did you—you got this from Karina down in the Looking Glass shop. *Look* at you!"

Penny brushed a nervous hand down the gown and nodded. "She was so nice. I rented it, I could never afford it, but it's so pretty...?" She glanced up at Ashley like she actually needed the reassurance.

Ashley spluttered. "Gorgeous. Perfect. Incredible. Beautiful. Look at you!" she said again.

The gown didn't, actually, clash with Penny's hair. In fact, it couldn't have been more suited to Penny's red hair and golden undertones if Karina had made it for her on purpose. It had an autumn motif, an uncountable number of individual soft embroidered leaves trimmed with gold and copper and layered on top of each other in playful lines, like they'd really been caught from a falling tree. There were glimpses of still-rich summer green, and hints of clear autumn yellow, and it all flowed like the wind was catching it even when the air was still. It clung to her curves without overwhelming her, and she'd had her jaw-length hair done in short Vikings-style braids that skimmed the sides of her head and gave the top of her hair height. But they weren't smooth: they were wild and ragged, woven with leaves and twigs, until the drummer looked like she'd stepped out of an autumn windstorm.

"You look like a dryad," Ashley said joyfully. "Like a wood sprite who's just *daring* a woodcutter to chop down her trees! Oh my God, no wonder Laurie told me I had to get dressed up. I should have done better than this, though, this is just, like…*me*, but Ren Faire."

"You're an elf princess," Penny blurted disbelievingly. "You look like an actual real life elf princess. I don't know why your ears aren't pointed. If this is just you, then you must be made completely of magic."

We are, Ashley's bear said happily. *You should tell her.*

Ashley almost wanted to, but the middle of a party

was just about the worst place she could think to do that. She shook her head, still beaming stupidly at Penny. "No, I'm just me. This isn't anything new or special."

"It's new and special for me to see you in it!"

"Oh, well." Her smile got even dumber, if that was possible. "Okay, I guess when you put it that way. Penny, you must have spent all afternoon getting ready for this. You're incredible. I don't even care if the whole thing is a terrible disaster now."

Penny laughed. "Yes, you do. But yes, I did, and yes, I am, so let's go enjoy it and make sure it's not a terrible disaster and show off our efforts, okay? Gwen's over there talking to Maggie Ross, who is even taller than you are. How many women have you met who are taller than you are?"

"Um." Ashley let Penny take her hand and draw her across the increasingly-crowded venue while she thought about that. "In the grand scheme of things, hardly any, I guess. I can think of quite a few right now but there obviously aren't nearly as many of them as there are women who are shorter than me. Oh gosh." Ashley stopped dead several feet from the professional wrestler, so suddenly and completely that Penny sort of bounced at the end of her arm and sprang back to Ashley's side.

"I told you she was tall," Penny whispered with a kind of triumph.

It was true. Maggie Ross was at least four inches taller than Ashley, even though Ashley was still wearing the thick-soled clogs she'd had on at work. The professional wrestler towered above everybody in the room except Ashley's cousin Bill, who, with his pompadour, almost matched her height. She was so blonde her hair, worn in a loose braid down her back, was nearly white, and her pale skin was pink from cold where her long, hippie-style fringed leather coat didn't protect her from the winter air. She didn't dress anything like what Ashley imagined a professional wrestler would. All her clothes had a definite hippie vibe, and were pastels and soft fabrics that looked comfortable and lovely.

But above and beyond all that, Maggie Ross was a *shifter*. And so was the slight, wolfish man at her side who gazed up at her with absolute adoration. Ashley sort of recognized him: Conri Lyell, the head of the All-Arena Entertainment group. He was clearly a predator, probably a wolf, from the lean look of him, but Maggie…

Ashley had absolutely no idea what she was, except whatever it was, was huge. She didn't feel like a polar bear or any other arctic predator Ashley could think of, but the female shifter's presence was so enormous that Ashley couldn't imagine Maggie was anything *but* a predator. She could knock somebody down just by looking at them!

Maggie turned her head to meet Ashley's eyes with her own cool blue gaze, and the ruff on her bear's neck stood straight up. *Do we fight?*

The answer to that was obviously no. Ashley was

still having a hard time telling *herself*, never mind her *bear*, that, when Maggie Ross grinned, a huge bright welcoming smile, and winked at Ashley. "You must be another Torben," she said over the heads of almost everybody standing between them, including her own husband. "Apparently you're the only family that grows them life-sized around here."

A huge rush of tension fizzled out of Ashley in a breath, and when Maggie just basically reached out above everybody else's head to shake her hand, Ashley took it. "Hi. Yes, I'm Ashley Torben, and this is my—friend—Penny. It's great to meet you, Ms. Ross."

"Maggie," the other tall woman said cheerfully. "This is my husband Conri. We understand you came to the rescue when the original event venue burned down, so thank you. I was looking forward to this. Swans are a pet project of mine."

There was no way this woman, six foot eight in heels, was a swan part of the time. That, Ashley thought, would be absolutely terrifying. "I really didn't do anything. It was my cousin Laurie's idea, and then Penny had everything to make it work. She's the one who saved the day."

Maggie stepped through the crowd effortlessly to find Penny and offer her a hand, too. "Well, thanks to you, then. You..." Her incredibly pale eyebrows drew down as she examined Penny, who was literally fifteen inches shorter than she was. "We, ah, we don't run in the same circles, do we? Mile high club sorts of things?"

Penny's eyebrows flew up. "Um! No! I don't think

so! It's a very nice offer but you're married and I'm dating Ashley here!"

The tall shifter blinked, then burst out laughing. "Right, yes, sorry. Excuse me. Don't know what I was thinking. Anyway, it's really nice to meet you, and seriously, thanks for rescuing this event. Thanks. Usually we go to all these boring business meetings for stuff Conri does. This is much more my speed."

"Yes," Conri said from somewhere behind her, "you have such a difficult time lying on the beach while I sit around in stuffy buildings trying to get people to agree to non-exorbitant rates for hotels and arenas."

"He's lying," Maggie said in a terrible *sotto voce*. "I can put on SunBlock Ten Thousand and still burn if I lie on a beach for more than ninety seconds. Stick around," she added. "There's supposed to be a visiting swan later tonight. Tame, apparently." She winked at Ashley again, and went back to meeting-and-greeting the crowd around them.

Penny clutched Ashley's arm and dragged her far enough away to not be overheard. "Did she just proposition *both* of us? She kept winking at you and what was that about the mile high club!"

Ashley stared toward the wrestler for a few more seconds, then shook her head. She was now almost certain the woman *was* a swan shifter, and out loud, said, "No, she couldn't have been. Swans are monogamous. So are wolves, for that matter."

"What?"

"Uh. Nothing. No, I don't think she was propositioning you, but..." Ashley trailed off, gazing down at Penny in confusion, then shrugged it off. "No, I don't have any idea what that was about. Unless you actually fly a lot?"

Penny snorted. "We don't even have a tour *bus*, never mind a tour *plane*. We drive around in a 1970s van like a bunch of Scoobies."

"Yeah, then I don't know. Never mind," Ashley said firmly. "I have to be in and out to check the pub for emergencies, but I've still got a few minutes here. Should we check out what they've done with the place?"

"Ah, yes." Penny dropped into a soothing nature-documentarian-type voice as they wandered around the tents. "Here we have Holidayus Erroneous, where two or more young people are making a drunken holiday decision they'll be regretting in the morning. Over there you'll see the less-common Partyous Pooperous, who disapproves of anyone having fun at a holiday gathering. But here we have the extraordinarily common yet much-beloved..." She went on, sometimes drowned out by Ashley's giggling, and leaned on Ashley as they stopped to watch a group of young women in elaborate Renaissance Faire garb dancing. A number of young men joined them, and Ashley suddenly gave a braying laugh.

"Oh, no. They're nine ladies dancing and ten lords a-leaping. Count them."

"I can't, they won't hold still!" Penny laughed, though, as she realized Ashley was right. "Please tell me they're not going to have six geese a-laying around here. Oh my god, though, they *do* have the drummers and the pipers. I thought they were flautists!"

Ashley, in as severe a tone as she could manage, said, "If you're going to flautist, go to the bathroom," then giggled proudly at herself as Penny first gave her a look much more severe than her tone had been, then dissolved into her own giggles.

"So what I've learned on this important first date—"

"Second, or I can't bring you to the family reunion on Tuesday—"

"This important *second* date is that you have a juvenile sense of humor. Which is excellent, because I've long suspected myself of being a twelve year old at heart. I wouldn't have thought it of you, though. You're so tall and elegant."

"Tall people can't be twelve at heart?" Ashley asked, amused.

"Well, when you say it like that it sounds ridiculous, but from down here in the trenches where I'm the height of the average twelve year old girl, it seems more *like* I should be and you shouldn't, right?"

"See," Ashley said wryly, "that's one of the things that actually sucks about being tall. They figure you're older and therefore more mature than you are. Maybe I never really got to revel in my inner tweenage idiot."

Penny made a show of looking for Ashley's cousins. "With *those* two around?"

Ashley grimaced dramatically. "Yeah, okay, fair, you

called that one. Sometime I'll tell you about the Disney-land Incident."

A slow grin stretched across Penny's face. "Now is sometime."

Ashley laughed and shook her head. "No. I'm still in the 'trying to make a good impression' stages here."

"Excuse me, I have to go talk to a man about a water barrel." Penny headed toward Laurie until Ashley collared her and pulled her back. The petite drummer's eyes widened a bit and went dark with an intent interest that took Ashley's breath away. She hadn't exactly meant to get all raar and pushy, but it appeared Penny might like that kind of thing. She was warm and soft and had pulled herself right up against Ashley, all at once, murmuring, "Or not," breathlessly. "Seems like you might have something better in mind."

Take our mate to your den right now, Ashley's bear said enthusiastically. *She wants to go to the den right now!*

It was hard to argue with that. Ashley couldn't think of much better to do with her time, either, except the fact that she was very much still at work and had just spent the afternoon yelling at her cousins for blowing off their shifts. So all she could really risk right then was ducking her head toward Penny's and whispering, "I've got a whole list."

To her surprise, Penny threw her head back and laughed unexpectedly. "Of course you do. A list. I bet you've got an actual list somewhere, too, don't you? You're so organized."

Embarrassed laughter crawled through Ashley. "I don't have an *actual* list…"

"Okay, no, no, you've probably got a hundred neatly filed bookmarks under a private tab in your phone, and a checkbox to go through and try the things that look most intriguing." Penny's eyebrows rose challengingly. "Am I wrong?"

Ashley, blushing furiously, said, "I'm not going to dignify that with an answer."

"I cannot *wait* to earn your phone password," Penny said gleefully. "You're wonderful."

Still blushing, but suddenly almost wistful, Ashley said, "Am I?"

Penny gave her an incredulous look, then, still smiling but no longer laughing, threaded her hands up into Ashley's hair and pulled her down for a kiss.

CHAPTER 12

Ashley's mouth was warm and so soft, and smiling. A little surprised smile against Penny's mouth that fell away as the sweet kiss lingered. Ashley put her hands on Penny's waist, and Penny had the heady certainty that the tall woman could pick her up easily. The thought made her giggle with anticipation, and Ashley broke away, smiling at her again from up close. "Are you laughing at me?"

"I'm laughing at the idea of having such a nice tall girlfriend," Penny admitted. "I mean, sorry to escalate, but—"

"I like escalation." Ashley's voice did that thing again where it dipped unexpectedly low, into the 'listen to her read a phone book' range again, and Penny shivered.

"I would escalate you right out of here if we both weren't working."

Ashley blinked, then straightened to stare toward

the stage with a sheepish look. "Oh right. I'd almost convinced myself it would be worth my cousins' wrath if I just snuck off with you. I forgot you were playing tonight." She looked back down at Penny, unexpected shyness in her brown eyes. "There's probably some stuff I should tell you before we sneak off, anyway."

Penny waved a hand. "Ill-considered college liaisons with incredibly inappropriate people? We've all been there. A phase where you tried to convince yourself you really *were* into boys? I—"

"No," Ashley said firmly. "No, absolutely not. Ew."

Penny laughed. "Oh. Well, I was going to say I'm bi, so I have sympathy for the impulse, but never mind."

"I'm amazed some good-looking rock god hasn't snatched you up, then," Ashley said, sounding like she meant it.

"Eh." Penny glanced around, gestured toward a bench that had just emptied, and pulled Ashley over to curl up against her there. "The last good-looking rock god I dated was more like a rock frog. The truth is the Sixty Pix have been verging on something big for a while and guys could see it and they'd get jealous. They wanted me to be in *their* band, or to just quit doing music at all and stay home and have kids. I love kids," Penny admitted wistfully. "I'd love to have them. But I'm never gonna be the one who stays at home even if I had them, and a lot of guys still really don't like that. Oooh." She made a face, hearing herself. "Wow, I'm just laying the dealbreaker topics out right from the start, aren't I?"

Ashley said, "There are no dealbreaker topics," with such soft conviction that Penny's heart flipped.

"You can't know that," Penny said weakly. "I might… I don't know. Do something really awful."

"Do you leave the toilet seat up in the middle of the night so I'll fall in?"

"No!!"

"Then we're good," Ashley said with that same determination, although she was smiling now, obviously trying to be more light-hearted. "No, I mean, of course, you're right, you could do something awful—"

"Oh, so now you think I'm an awful person."

"Hey!" Ashley laughed. "Hey, that's not fair!"

"I know," Penny said cheerfully. "But being a not-fair dork is probably better than throwing dealbreaker topics into second dates. Sorry, I have no idea why I'm getting so intense." She did, of course. Ashley focused, dedicated, intelligent, gorgeous, funny, kind, and didn't brook fools easily, and Penny had been pretending not to nurse a crush on her for two months now. "But I like spending time with you," she added more quietly. "Even if I'm being kind of an idiot about it."

"I'm the one who was so afraid to talk to you I avoided Gwen and Bill for a week," Ashley said.

Penny sat up, jaw falling open. "What? Is that why you didn't hang out with us that first week we were in Renaissance after the gigs?" At Ashley's embarrassed nod, Penny burst into laughter and opened her arms, offering the tall woman a hug. "That's adorable," she said into Ashley's shoulder. "And makes me feel better.

I thought it was me, because I knew you'd been hanging out with Gwen before I got there. Okay, subject change: I know it was my idea to sit down, but it turns out if I stop moving I'll freeze to death, so, do you dance?"

Ashley winced like it came from the bottom of her soul. "Badly."

"Excellent. Me too. Let's go join the nine dancing ladies and ten leaping lords." Somehow, the strapping young men in Renaissance-lord sorts of costumes were still managing to leap, even though quite a lot of people had joined the nine dancing ladies on the dance floor. Mostly the young men were leaping up and down, not out or across, which helped, but if Penny had tried that, she would have landed on peoples' feet.

It turned out neither of them were lying: she and Ashley were *not* good dancers, but Ashley caught Penny's hand and spun her around like a top until they were both giggling again, and then the drummers and pipers played a slower tune that let them snuggle up together and compliment each other on how bad they were at dancing. "I'm going to have to go back in soon," Ashley said reluctantly. "I have to at least go check up on things in the pub."

"I know. No rest for the wicked. Oh no, now what?"

Someone was getting up on stage to make an announcement, and the party quieted down a bit as a cheerfully round man with fluffy white hair said, "In the spirit of the Twelve Days of Christmas theme, we considered releasing a barnyard full of birds and having an old-fashioned greased-pig style contest, but after careful consideration, we decided to accept five golden rings as prizes from various sponsors. The rings have been hidden around the venue. Put five bucks in the donation pot and join the treasure hunt!"

"I can't," Ashley said woefully. "I really have to go in."

"I'll put ten in and look for you," Penny promised. "Think you'll be able to come back out later?"

"Well, I hear the Sixty Pix are playing later tonight, and I think the drummer is hot, so yeah, I guess I'd better." Ashley smiled down at Penny, then with a regretful sigh, hurried out of the event tents and back to the main pub.

"I'll find you that ring!" Penny shouted after her. Ashley waved, and Penny went to put a tenner in the pot and joined Gwen and Bill as they poked around the venue. Somebody shouted in triumph as they found the first ring. Applause and cheers rose, then twice more in the next few minutes as the next two were found, but the last two were apparently better-hidden, and most people lost interest. It was at least half an hour later that somebody else shouted with surprise and another cheer went up, but the last ring still hadn't been found when Maggie Ross got up on stage and made a speech thanking people for turning up to the charity event.

"A lot of you probably know something about the history of conservation for swans, since you're here supporting this event, but did you know that in the 1930s, there were fewer than a hundred known specimens of trumpeter swans left in the United States? The species was saved when they found a huge native population in Alaska and reintroduced them across the rest of the nation. We can't rely on luck like that for our conservation efforts." She went on for a few minutes, speaking passionately, then ended with a smiling, "I know we're not specifically here to raise funds for trumpeters, but they're the heaviest bird native to North America, and we do have one to introduce to you this evening. Conri and I are going to go get her, and while she *is* fairly tame and patient, please remember that she's also a wild animal and you probably shouldn't behave like idiots around her."

Laughter and promises rose with the applause, and Ashley snuck back into the charity event a few minutes before Conri Lyell walked in with what had to be the world's largest swan on a very fancy leash.

A genuine gasp ran around the gathering, and people actually stepped back, clearing a path for the huge bird. Penny, looking between her own heeled shoes and the top of the swan's head, whispered, "That thing is *literally* bigger than I am, holy shit! Like she's got to be at least two inches taller than me!"

"Only if you count the neck," Ashley said in a high thin voice that sounded like she was trying to fight off laughter.

"Obviously I count the neck! Its eyes are higher than mine! I didn't know swans got that big!"

A lot of people were whispering similar things, and as Conri led the swan up onto the stage where she could be admired, he said, "They generally don't," in a wry tone. "Even the largest swans are usually only about four feet high at the top of their heads. This one is a showoff."

The swan turned her head to, by all appearances, give Conri a dirty look. Laughter splashed across the venue again and people took pictures, expressing their awe and, when Conri led the swan down again, approaching nervously to see if they could stroke her soft feathers. Penny whispered, "She's very patient," and Ashley said, "Oh you have *no* idea," in that same voice that struggled against laughter. "I'd bite somebody if they tried doing that to me."

"Good thing you're not a giant swan, then," Penny said ruefully, and for some reason Ashley dissolved into laughter, to the point of actually having to sit and put her face in her hands while she giggled.

"I'll explain later," she promised. "I will, but right now, just trust me, that's funny."

Penny eyed her. "If you say so. I'm going to go pet the swan." She all but tip-toed up to the bird, who turned its elegant head toward her and tilted it as if studying Penny carefully. Then she looked at Penny from the other eye, as if really trying to get her measure, and finally extended her beak to press it against Penny's chest.

Actually, to poke her. With enough force that Penny lurched a step back, regained her feet, and glared at the huge bird. "Hey! Be polite! I was being nice!"

The swan fluffed its feathers, which made everyone except Penny take several judicious steps backward.

She had the absolutely irrational confidence she could take this beast, or at least, that she shouldn't take it being rude to her, and stuck her fists on her hips defiantly.

She swore to god the swan actually laughed at her. It opened its mouth and made a deep *aah-oh!* sound right at her chest, then shook its feathers and did it again, more quietly and with what Penny honestly felt was amusement. She was still glaring at the big bird in confused irritation when it brushed past her, heading back out to whatever carrier it had been brought in. Conri Lyell widened his eyes at Penny as he went by. "I guess she liked you!"

"That's a weird way to show it!" Penny scurried back to Ashley, who had stood up and was leaning, almost scowling, after the swan, as if she'd been afraid she would have to teach the huge bird a lesson. "I'm fine," Penny promised in a mutter. "That was just weird."

"I've never seen anything like it." Ashley put her hands on Penny's shoulders, looking her over like the swan had actually assaulted her. "You're okay?"

"I'm sort of rattled, but yeah, otherwise fine. It's okay. I'll take it out on the drums." Penny arched her eyebrows toward the stage. "*After* everybody is done throwing money at the charity because they got to see a humongous swan up close."

"You've got to give them credit for the fundraiser," Ashley agreed, still in a somewhat strained voice. "I think I really need to talk to you, Penny, although not until after work tonight."

Penny made a face. "Second date and we're already into the 'we have to talk' stuff, huh? Okay, well, assuming you haven't decided this is all a terrible idea—"

"I haven't."

"—then I'll just go up there and get all hot and sweaty and remind you why you like drummer girls. You do like drummer girls, right?"

Ashley smiled. "I never knew how much."

"Great. And then we can talk when you get off work." Penny made her way up to the stage, meeting Gwen at the edge and saying hi to Ripley, a local guitarist who had worked with Gwen before. Ripley had to be at least twenty-one, because otherwise they wouldn't be allowed into the pub to play. Penny thought they looked about seventeen and adorable, all shaggy hair and shapeless clothing and huge, awe-stricken eyes because the Sixty Pix were their favorite band. Getting up on stage with Gwen and the band was bucket list stuff for Ripley, and this wasn't even the first time Ripley had had the opportunity. Penny half expected they would eventually join the band, although somebody might have to retire for that to happen, and it certainly wasn't going to be her.

There was a gratifying shout of enthusiastic greeting as the three of them went up on stage. Gwen— who, despite her reluctance to step into the limelight, was *great* at it—shouted the band's hellos back at the crowd, laughing as Penny provided a drum sting to back it up. Something flew off the cymbal and Penny caught it without even seeing what it was, shoved it into her pocket for later as she fixed the screw on the cymbal, and lost herself in the beat for the next forty minutes or so.

It was a shock to come out of it. The end of a gig always felt so abrupt, even if they hung on for the encores and the cheering and everything else that might happen. Penny never wanted to leave the stage, and that larger-than-life feeling of exuberance and connection that the music, the drumming, carried with it.

Tonight, though, for the first time in ages, she had somebody waiting offstage for her. *That* feeling was something special, too. Penny took her bows, applauded both Gwen and Ripley, and went back down into the dispersing crowd to find the woman she hoped to call 'girlfriend' pretty soon.

CHAPTER 13

Ashley knew perfectly well that the swan had been Maggie Ross. She *didn't* know why Maggie had poked and prodded at *her* fated mate, and now that Penny had gone up on stage, Ashley was having a difficult time not stalking up to the professional wrestler and demanding to understand what was going on.

We can take her, Ashley's bear said placidly. *Swans are large, but we're larger. Much. Much. Larger.*

Much, Ashley agreed ferociously. Except in human form, Maggie was a solid four inches taller than Ashley, and considerably broader and more muscular. And also did stage fighting that required real skill for a living. Ashley was fairly confident that the professional wrestler could suplex her, and then probably tie her in knots and hang her from a tree.

Her bear produced a vivid image of swatting the swan shifter halfway across Renaissance, feathers flying everywhere. Despite her pique, Ashley ended up giggling. *Not unless we shift to bear form, and that would raise a lot more questions than it settled.*

Hnf. The bear offered another image of dragging Maggie off into the woods by her long neck so they could shift and put the big swan in her place out there.

"No," Ashley murmured, smiling again. "No, you're missing the point, you're missing the part where unless we're shifted, she can probably kick my ass."

Her bear made a dubious sound. *You're a very strong human.*

Yes, but so is she! We're both shifter-strong, but she's also a professional athlete! And she's bigger than me!

The bear said *hnf* again. *We could take her.*

"Or we could talk to her!" Ashley whispered. Fortunately the band was up on stage, greeting everybody and encouraging a lot of noise, so Ashley didn't sound like a total lunatic talking to herself. Or maybe she did, but nobody was likely to notice, which was more the point. She stretched her neck, looking for Maggie—as if, being the two tallest women and two of the tallest people at the event at all, it would be hard to see her—and when she didn't, settled back down a little. *Maybe we should just watch Penny perform.*

Yes, the bear said happily. *Watch everyone admire our mate.* After a pause, the bear, somewhat warily, added, *...our mate is very loud.*

That was true. There was no way around it. Penny made a hell of a lot of noise on those drums, but she did it with style. *We'll soundproof the garage so she can practice in there,* Ashley offered, and her bear settled down, satisfied with that idea, mostly because it had no idea Ashley didn't have a garage, just an apartment with a parking space below it.

Even with only two members of the band, and a local stand-in to help out, watching the Sixty Pix up on stage was an absolute joy. Penny and Gwen both obviously loved what they did, and Ripley, whom Ashley had known since they'd been a kid, was beaming like they'd been given Christmas and their birthday all at once. The audience loved them all, too, singing along, cheering when they didn't know the words, and dancing under the tents to keep warm. It was just about perfect, Ashley thought.

A few minutes into their set, she went reluctantly back into the pub, making sure nothing was on fire in there, either figuratively or literally. Jon grabbed her as soon as she came in, muttering an apology but explaining there was a patron looking for the manager. The patron, a man in his sixties who had been coming to the Thunder Bear for a long time, didn't like the new look, the new music, or the crowds, and felt he deserved the opportunity to tell somebody about that at length.

"I've been coming here as long as you've been alive," he told Ashley, "and you're ruining the place. Your aunt and uncle must be horrified. I expect things to change, young lady. The customer is always right."

"In matters of taste," Ashley said politely.

The older man frowned at her. "What?"

"The entire phrase is 'the customer is always right in matters of taste,' Mr Wilson."

"What the hell is that supposed to mean?"

"It means I would never argue with your tastes."

His eyebrows drew down in confusion. "So you're putting it back the way it was?"

"I wouldn't dream of it." Ashley gestured and began to walk the older man out, although he didn't realize it yet. It took him a moment to realize that she wasn't agreeing with him, and came to a belligerent stop.

"What do you mean? You just said the customer is always right!"

"See, the problem is that we've gotten used to the first half of that phrase being the end all and be all," Ashley said, still determined to be polite as she started walking again. Wilson had to scurry to catch up if he wanted to keep complaining to her, although she didn't give him much chance. "But in fact, the customer is wrong a lot of the time. In this case, you're specifically wrong about Aunt Heather and Uncle Pete being horrified, but in general, you're wrong that your personal preferences should dictate the direction a business you don't own should go in."

Wilson spluttered. "But I've been coming here for thirty years!"

Ashley beamed at him. "And we appreciate your patronage, and hope to see you back again as the Thunder Bear Brewpub embraces a new look and feel for the new year. Please, have a beer on the house the next time you come in." She handed him a coupon and walked him all the way into the parking lot, where she left him stammering with confused outrage.

"That," Jon said as she came back inside, "was awesome. Is that the new vibe around here? Escort entitled buttheads out and leave them confused in the cold?"

Ashley took a deep, deep breath. "I think it might be, yeah. I'm…" She pursed her lips, gazing around the busy pub. Between the two holiday parties and the youthful, cheerful crowd who had come in to fill the rest of the space, they were at pretty near capacity. Much, much busier than Sunday nights had been just a few months ago, with an entirely different crowd being catered to. The pub felt vibrant and alive, with the scent of food and beer both rising through the chatter and bursts of laughter.

"I'm not Bill," she said after a while. "He was trying so hard to keep things the same, to honor your mom and dad's legacy. It's really not his fault that the clientele was aging out, that they had other things to be doing, but he was afraid to change things and disappoint your folks. I came in with a whole new idea and laid it out to everybody when Bill offered me this job. I'm really not interested in pandering to the old crowd, which was diminishing anyway. So…yeah, I guess so. If anybody is going to be a dick about the direction we're taking the place, then they're not the clientele we want. I'm happy to show them the door."

"You're not worried about taking a hard line?"

"I don't think it's all that hard," Ashley admitted.

"But no, I guess I'm not. If there were only twelve people in here tonight and they were all sitting in a booth of their own, nursing a drink and sulking, then yeah, okay, I guess I'd be worried about the choices I was making for the business. But the place is packed, and that's not even including the insane last-minute party going on in the back lot. I get that right now it's Christmas, and I know that the last few months we've been riding on the high from having the Sixty Pix do such incredible gigs here in October, so things will probably calm down in the new year and it's going to take more work to get great nights like this going here. But unless it falls back to where it was, and falls *hard*, I think we're going to be just fine telling people like Mr Wilson that he can take his business elsewhere. And," she said with an upward flicker of her eyebrows, "I bet he won't anyway."

Jon's eyebrows rose too. "No?"

"Well, for one thing, I just offered him a free beer the next time he comes in. But also, he's been coming here for thirty years. This is his habit. I'm guessing he'll complain about it, but he'll come back."

"You're kind of ruthless, aren't you, Ash?"

Ashley grinned at her cousin. "Are you seriously only just now figuring that out?"

Jon drew, "Nooo" out, but his expression was curious. "I've just never seen it in action in the adult world, maybe. You used to run us ragged when we were kids, but somehow I didn't—" He broke off, laughing. "I didn't think of it as 'leadership skills' until just now, I guess. I just thought you were—"

Ashley held up a warning finger. "I'm sure you're not about to end that sentence with 'bossy.'"

Jon, who had obviously been about to end that sentence with 'bossy,' said, "—uh, pushy? Please don't hurt me." He mimed cringing away fearfully from a blow, and Ashley obligingly threatened him with one before he said, "It's good, though. You're good at this. Sorry again that Laurie and I have been making it harder. Speaking of which." He nodded back at the floor, and returned to work.

Ashley made sure there were no other crises going on, and made it out to the charity tents before the Sixty Pix quite finished up, so she was there to clap and cheer as the performers came off stage. Penny bounced toward her, shining both with enthusiasm and, as she'd warned earlier, sweat, and shied back from the hug that Ashley offered. "I'm much too disgusting right now. I'd stain your dress. As it is I'm going to have to pay for dry cleaning on this before I return it. I didn't think of that," she admitted as she gestured at the autumn-gold gown she'd rented. "But at least I looked pretty."

"You looked gorgeous," Ashley murmured. "You *look* gorgeous. Sweaty and all. You really come to life up there, don't you?"

"It's the best thing in the world," Penny said. "I love performing. I love drumming. I love my life, and," she said with a sudden violent shiver, "I love really big warm fluffy coats or going indoors because oh my god, the sweat drying on my skin is going to turn me into an icicle in about ninety seconds here. I didn't think it was that cold out until just now!"

"It's been that cold all along," Ashley promised. "You just weren't as, um, perspire-y."

"Sweaty," Penny said firmly. "There is no delicate word for the amount of sweat I work up on stage. And that's fine. There's nothing wrong with sweat. There is something wrong with freezing to death!"

"Right!" Ashley put her arm around Penny's shoulders and swept her toward the pub. "Do Gwen and Ripley need to be returned to warmth, too?"

Penny cast a look over her shoulder. "Bill's got Gwen taken care of, and Ripley wears much more sensible clothes than what I've got on right now. I think they'll be fine. I just need to dry off and put a coat on and I'll be okay too. Or I can stay inside and watch you rule the roost." She smiled up at Ashley as they went inside. "Which sounds pretty appealing, really. If I stay in here, nobody will recruit me to help clean up out there now that the party is over."

Ashley laughed. "I see how it is! I'm being used to avoid work!"

"Yeah," Penny said cheerfully. "I'll just pull up a bar stool, eat some cheese fries, and let everybody else do the heavy lifting. I couldn't risk this dress anyway."

"Cheese fries will be on the house," Ashley promised, and a few minutes later, Penny was indeed perched on a bar stool, nursing a beer and eating cheese fries while Sixty Pix fans stopped by to ask for pictures and autographs.

Our mate is popular, Ashley's bear said with great satisfaction. *She'll be good for you.*

Ashley blinked at the bear, vaguely offended. *Am I not popular?*

You take working very seriously. You should spend more time sunning and eating. Our mate will make sure you do that, because many people want to sun and eat with her and she'll want you to join her when they do.

"Oh," Ashley said out loud, glancing toward Penny again, and then, silently, *Oh, no. That whole life is way beyond me. I'm just a bar manager. I don't want to be famous.*

Are you going to let your mate eat all her meals with other people? the bear asked archly.

What? No!

Satisfaction radiated from the bear again. *Then you will spend more time relaxing, and that will be good.*

Ashley, with the sense that she had absolutely lost this argument, went back to work like that wasn't proving the bear's point.

CHAPTER 14

*P*enny was used to staying up late. It came with the job. On the other hand, she was also used to playing music until nearly midnight, and not coming down off that high until two or three in the morning. When the band got done at ten p.m., the performance rush ran out about midnight.

Unfortunately, the Thunder Bear Brewpub didn't stop serving alcohol until midnight on a Sunday, and it was another hour before the pub fully closed. By that time, Penny was nearly asleep on the bar counter, having long since finished her fries and having made the in-retrospect-terrible decision to have a second beer. She propped her chin on her hand, watching sleepily as the bar got cleaned up around her. Ashley managed to look elegant and not get dirt on that gorgeous green elfin dress even as she mopped the floor and cleaned up spilled beer here and there.

It was kind of fun to watch the clean-up crew. They worked together with the efficiency of long-familiar, well-rehearsed efforts, with tired but light-hearted banter bouncing around the otherwise-quiet pub. It was such a comfortable, friendly space: log-cabin style walls, deep booths with leather seat covers and polished brass knobs, gleaming wooden tables both in the booths and standing free around the floor. There were American and state flags hanging high on the walls and in the rafters, and various Pride flags had joined them since the first time Penny had been in the pub. There were small snowdrifts built up against the winter-dark windows, which reflected warm yellow light back into the pub. It was a homey space, warm and comforting and welcoming.

"Pen?" A hand touched Penny's shoulder and she jolted awake, startled and checking to see if she needed to wipe drool off her face, or worse, off the bar.

Ashley was grinning at her, if a grin could be soft and gentle as well as brightly wicked. "You lost it in the last ten minutes," she told her. "I watched your head slide down your arm and hit the bar in slow motion. Can I drive you home?"

Penny dragged in a breath to protest, then thought about getting in her cold, cold van and driving back to the hotel, and nodded. "I think so, yeah, please. But you wanted to talk!"

The fondness stayed in Ashley's smile. "It can wait until you're not falling asleep on the bar, I promise."

"I bet I won't be sleepy anymore once I go outside into the, what's the temperature? Seventeen degrees?"

"We'll pretend it's that warm," Ashley said, amused. "Do you have a coat, or were you afraid of crushing that amazing dress?"

"Right, that'll wake me right up. My coat is in the van." Penny made a face. "Where it's probably turned to an icicle, too."

Ashley laughed. "I'll lend you mine."

"Your dress is not any warmer than mine is."

"No, but I run warm. I'll be fine, honestly."

"I'll probably also step on the hem of your coat." Penny gestured to the difference in their heights as she slipped off the bar stool, and Ashley laughed again.

"It's thigh length on me, so it'll probably hit your ankles. You'll be cute."

"Probably," Penny said in mock despair. "Cute is the bane of short women. Although if I'm being honest, there are much worse things than being cute. All right, if you're sure you won't freeze."

"I'm sure." Ashley got her coat from the staff room, waving Penny over so she could wrap it around her and grin down at her. "I'm right. You're really cute."

Penny, from within a fluffy warm hood and a hem that did in fact reach her ankles, said, "I feel ridiculous and yet adorable."

"That's exactly what you are. Okay, we're the last ones in the building. Ready to make a break for it?" Ashley grabbed her hand and they ran from the pub, although the headlong exit stopped immediately outside the front door, partly because Ashley needed to lock up, and partly because although the parking lot was pretty well cleared, it was also winter in Colorado and ice was a thing. They were much more careful approaching Ashley's car, which, to Penny's delight, was warmed up and defrosted. "Oh," Ashley said brightly, "didn't I tell you I've got an automatic starter?"

"And to think I even considered taking my van!" Penny bundled into the car, trying to see around the edges of the hood, and finally fell into the passenger seat with a laugh. "This hood is deep enough for two of me. I feel like I'm seven."

"You don't look like you are." Ashley's warm voice warmed up even more, and Penny felt a blush rising as the taller woman leaned forward and peered through the windshield. "If you're awake enough, it looks like we might be getting some Northern Lights. We could drive out of town a ways and see if we can get a good view?"

"Oh, yes!" Penny sat up from where she'd been nestling into the blessedly heated seat. "No one should ever be too tired to go stand around in the freezing cold and stare at the dancing lights in the sky for a while."

Ashley chuckled as she drove them out of the parking lot. "A woman after my own heart. Did you talk to Maggie Ross again?"

"The wrestler? No, she disappeared after the swan visit. Actually, before it, I think. I assume she waited back at the car to load that ginormous thing back in again. It's a good way to slip out without people mobbing you."

"Sounds like you know something about it."

Penny turned her head against the window, smiling at the streetlight-illuminated darkness as it slipped by. "Yes, but I don't mean it in a bad way. Some days you really want to get down into the grind with the fans and others, no matter how high you are from the performance, you just need some space to breathe. And the Sixty Pix aren't nearly as famous as Maggie Ross is. Well, Gwen is, but she's different."

She heard Ashley's quick smile in the other woman's voice. "Is that weird? You don't have to answer, obviously, but is it weird?"

"No. Yes. Totally. Not at all." Penny laughed and turned her gaze to Ashley's smiling profile. "Ninety percent of the time, ninety-five percent of the time, it's extremely normal and not weird at all. The other five or ten percent it is *crazy* weird. Gwen's very chill about it, except she's also not. Everything with her dad, with really her whole childhood, she really doesn't make a big deal about it. She never has. Myles, our bassist, actually didn't know until this *year* that she'd been a child star, and he's been with the band for years. But when she has to deal with it, she's either really cool and open and relatable or she's an absolute ice queen bitch demon about her privacy. She's legit inspiring."

"Did you know who she was when you joined the band?"

Penny gave an ungainly snort. "I recognized her

when I went into the audition and nearly peed myself." Ashley laughed out loud, and Penny went on, raising her voice a bit until Ashley's laughter died down. "But I tried not to freak out and I guess I succeeded, because she didn't realize I'd recognized her for a couple years and we've been pretty much BFFs for almost as long as I can remember, now."

"That's wonderful." Ashley cast her an incredibly sweet smile. "I was always best friends with my zillions of boy cousins. It must be nice to have a best girl friend."

"It is. You'll love her too," Penny promised. "Actually, she thinks you're amazing anyway, so, yeah. Oooh." She leaned forward, catching a glimpse of green in the sky as they left the city lights behind. "Oh, it's going to be a good show tonight!"

"There's a parking lot for a hiking trail right up ahead," Ashley said. "We're not supposed to go up on the trail in the middle of the night, obviously—"

"And we're not exactly dressed for it," Penny said wryly.

Ashley blinked between them, and laughed. "Right. No, we're not. So we'll stay in the parking lot, but the view should be pretty good there. Especially if the lights are out."

"It looks like enough of them are," Penny reported a moment later as they climbed the road toward the lot. "As for the rest, well, I've got a mean throwing arm."

"Penny!" Ashley sounded genuinely shocked.

"I wouldn't!" Penny paused. "I totally would. As long as there were no security cameras."

"There aren't," Ashley said, sounding unexpectedly confident. "People in Renaissance aren't big on surveillance."

"Well, then." Penny mimed warming her throwing arm up, and Ashley gave her another dubious, shocked look. "Okay, I won't! Not if you're going to look all moral and conflicted at me!" They tumbled out of the car into the frigid air, both of them looking skyward at the columns of green stretching across the sky. Penny shivered happily. "Oh, that's perfect. Look at that. It's been a good year for the lights."

"Lots of sunspot activity." Ashley, tentatively, slipped her hand into Penny's, and Penny nestled up close, smiling as they watched the sky for several minutes.

Then, abruptly, Penny realized *she* was shivering, and Ashley wasn't wearing a coat at all. "Oh my God. We have to get back in the car. You're going to die of hypothermia."

"I'm honestly okay. No hypothermia, no frostbite. Here, see?" Ashley put her fingers against Penny's cheek, where they felt like heating elements warming her skin.

"That's crazy," Penny said breathlessly. "How are you doing that?"

Ashley hesitated. "I can tell you, but it's kind of a… it's crazy. It's a lot. It might be more than you want to know."

"Oh no. I want to know. I wish to master this strange ability."

"I don't think you can," Ashley said sheepishly. "It's innate to me. To my kind of people."

Penny's eyebrows crawled upward. "To tall blondes?"

"No." Ashley laughed. "No, although my whole family can do it. Um. Okay, you, I, I need to step back."

"Sure, that's fine, I'll just go over here and shiver." Penny took a few steps away, speaking in her most pathetic voice.

Ashley eyeballed her. "That isn't fair."

"No, it wasn't. Sorry. Go on, tell me what this thing is."

"I really have to show you. Because I'll say it and you won't believe it. So this is me saying it." Ashley swallowed nervously. "I can shapechange. I can shapeshift into a bear."

"Okay, that's a brand-new weird one on me," Penny announced. "I don't even know what that's supposed to mean. Is it code for something?"

Ashley, still visibly nervous, shook her head. "No. No, it's just…well…watch."

She took another step back, and then two more, before she shapeshifted into a bear. A huge, fluffy, golden-brown grizzly bear whose expression was somehow identical to the nervous look Ashley had had on her face. On her human face. Because she was a bear now. She had just shapeshifted, right there in front of Penny. That was a thing that had happened.

Penny looked around in her brain for a response, because screaming and running away seemed obvious, or maybe fainting, or maybe peeing herself, but none of those things seemed to be happening in her head.

Instead, a small bright voice somewhere in the back of her mind said, *I can do that!* and Penny shapeshifted into a partridge.

CHAPTER 15

Ashley shifted back to human and yelled, "Holy shit!" at the small, extremely startled-looking partridge in the snowbank a few feet away from her. "Holy shit, Penny, what the hell!? You just turned into a partridge!"

This is not supposed to go this way, her bear said, flabbergasted. *Our **mate** is supposed to be the one who shouts and is surprised!*

Our mate wasn't supposed to turn into a partridge! Ashley yelled back, although she tried to keep the yelling inside her head. Not very successfully, apparently, because the poor partridge—Penny—flapped her wings and fluttered back in alarm at all the noise Ashley was making. Then it dumped itself wing-first into the snowdrift, panicked, and started beating its wings even harder.

"Penny! Oh my God! Penny! Calm down! It's okay! Holy shit!" Ashley hurried forward to try to collect the panicked partridge in her arms. Penny started beating her wings harder and rose a few inches into the air, then let out a horrified squawk and collapsed into the drift, quivering with terror. Ashley, trying to sound calm and trustworthy, managed to drop her voice into a croon. "Hey, it's okay, baby. It's all right. I've got you, Penny. It's me, Ashley. I'm going to pick you up, okay? Don't scratch me. It's okay. Yeah, see, there? Everything is okay, baby."

The partridge did not look like everything was okay. On the other hand, she didn't fight or claw or flap any more as Ashley brought her arms down slowly and gently to scoop her up. "There," Ashley murmured. "There we go. That's it. That's all right. I've got you now. You're safe. Can you hear me, Penny? I want you to think about being human again, okay? You can just shift right back as easy as you shifted to being a bird. It's okay, just—oh! Oof!"

She went down into the snow with a thump as Penny *did* shift back: an armful of woman weighed a lot more than an armful of bird did. For a moment snow and her gown and cloak and everything flew every-where, settling with Penny's weight in Ashley's lap. She was warm and soft and smelled mostly wonderful, although there was a tang of sweat and possibly panic to her scent just then. "Good. Good job, that was good, you—"

"Oh my God!" Penny wailed. "What happened to my *clothes?*"

Ashley looked down at the woman in her arms. The

very, very *naked* woman in her arms. Penny's skin was already turning blue from the cold, her shoulders covered in goosebumps. The rest of her probably was too, but she was crunched up in Ashley's arms, shivering, and there wasn't much else visible as she huddled against Ashley's warmth.

Ashley's brain sputtered and so did her voice, a short series of attempted explanations that didn't get any farther than consonant sounds in the back of her throat. Then she managed the one word that really mattered: "*Car.*"

It wasn't easy standing up with a small ball of woman in her arms. Her bear said, *I could help!*, but Ashley shook her head as she staggered to her feet. It wasn't Penny's weight that was a problem; it was just that sitting cross-legged with someone bundled up against her was an awkward way to start, and the fact that she really, really didn't want to put Penny down in the snow. After a couple of attempts, she managed to scramble to her feet without dropping her poor shivering mate and hurried to the car, saying, *I think shifting to a bear underneath her is more than she could handle right now,* apologetically to her bear.

The bear rumbled a reluctant agreement as Ashley managed to get the car door open and to not-quite dump Penny into the passenger seat. "Hang on. I've got winter gear in the trunk." She closed the door, turned the car on with the remote starter, and got the coats, snow pants, and boots out of the car's trunk before crawling into the driver's seat. "Okay. Here you go. It's going to be fine, Penny. C'mon, let me help you get these on."

Penny was balled up in the passenger's seat as small as she could go, which was pretty small. Ashley tilted her away from the seat enough to drag the coat around her shoulders, and all of a sudden, in a scramble, Penny pulled it on and yanked the snow pants on before balling up in the seat again. "What happened to my *clothes*? What happened to me? What happened to *you!* What's going *on?*"

Those were all excellent questions, and Ashley barely knew where to start. She said, "This isn't typical," in a sort of high funny voice, and Penny's head popped out of the hood to yell, "You *think?*"

Ashley winced and Penny's expression crumpled into near-tears. "I'm sorry."

"No. No, baby, it's okay. It's, this is insane. This must be insane for you. Look, do you think we could crawl into the back seat? I think maybe you need some hugs while I explain this and it's hard to hug across a gear shift."

Penny, with a sniffle, said, "This is an automatic," but crawled into the back seat over what was, in fact, not a gear shift at all. Technically it was the storage compartment between the two front seats, but it had been a gear shift in Ashley's first car, and apparently she still thought that's what that space should hold.

That was probably more than she needed to explain to Penny right now. Especially since there was quite a lot else to explain to her. Ashley crawled into the back seat after her, and offered a tentative arm to hide in. Penny, wide-eyed and obviously stressy, shook her head, and Ashley nodded gently. "That's okay. Okay. First, you're a shifter, Penny."

Penny, hollowly, said, "'Yer a wizard, Harry,'" and shivered. "What does that mean? I'm a shifter. What does that mean? You turned into a *bear*."

"I did. I'm also a shifter. But I grew up knowing I was one, and you clearly didn't. That's..." Ashley took a deep breath. "That's very unusual. But we'll come back to that, okay? One thing at a time."

Penny's high-pitched laugh filled the car. "Sure. Right. One thing at a time. What happened to my clothes?"

That was as good a 'one thing' to start with as any. Ashley gave her mate a weak smile. "Usually when we shift, our clothes come and go with us. Anything touching our skin. Glasses, earrings, clothes, shoes, whatever. But it's something we learn when we're babies, like being potty trained, so we don't have to think about it when we're even just a little bit older. You've never shifted before, I guess, so you don't have that practice. So your clothes are..." She winced. "Gone."

"But I rented that dress!" Penny's voice rose even farther. "Can I get them back? If I, I, if I shift again and, and I don't know, call them? Will they come back?"

"I don't know," Ashley said slowly. "When young shifters forget their clothes, that's it, they're gone. But I don't know that a toddler could understand the idea of going to get the clothes they left behind."

"Well, could you?" Penny demanded.

"I—I've never tried. I've never forgotten my clothes. I can try. But not here, I can't shift in the car, I'll explode it." Ashley laughed out loud suddenly, all too aware it was the wrong moment, but reminded of something. "Poor Bill, he shifted in a Honda Civic once, and he's *huge*. I mean I'm big but he's *huge*. Now he drives a monster truck because he's afraid of getting stuck like that again."

"*Bill is a bear, too?*" Penny's voice shot up again. "And Gwen knows? And didn't tell me?"

"Well, we don't..." Ashley smiled with consternation. "We don't usually tell people who aren't... intimate..."

"You told me! We're not intimate!" Penny hesitated. "Yet?"

This, Ashley thought, was much, much more difficult than just telling a regular true human about fated mates. She said, "Yet," a little faintly, and tried to figure out where to go from there. Penny just sat there, staring at her with huge eyes, looking so lost and afraid and confused that all Ashley wanted to do was pull her close and promise it would all be okay. "Look, I'm just going to lay it all out, okay? This is way more complicated than I expected and we'll figure it all out, but let me at least tell you why I *was* telling you, because...I think I should," she finished awkwardly.

Penny made a small gesture that more said 'okay,

whatever' than showed any enthusiasm for the idea, but Ashley couldn't blame her. The poor drummer had just turned into a partridge, for God's sake. Adults didn't just randomly discover they were shifters. Usually that kind of thing hit at puberty if they didn't already know, and that was hard enough.

"Okay. Intimate. Um. So I'm a shifter, and one of the things about shifters is when we meet the person we're meant to be with, we know right away. We call it fate." Ashley hesitated. "You're my fated mate, Penny. Usually our mates are either other shifters, who know about it already, or true humans who have a shock to get over, but they adapt very fast. In this case..." She wet her lips. "In this case I don't know why you didn't already know you were a shifter. I don't even know why I couldn't tell you were OH MY GOD, Maggie Ross knew!"

Penny shrank down into the seat, all wide eyes and confusion from within the over-sized winter coat. "Maggie Ross? What does she have to do with..." Her eyes closed and after a heartbeat she said, "She was the swan. The gigantic swan?"

"I don't know how she knew!" Ashley half-yelled, struggling and failing to bring her voice down. "But she *knew* what the hell how did *she* know about my fated mate when *I* didn't maybe it's because she's a bird shifter oh my *god*! Oh my God! Okay!" She clutched the sides of her own head, trying to calm herself. "Okay. I'm sorry. Okay. The thing is, shifters can usually sense each other. But shifters also usually know they're shifters, so...I don't know, Penny. Maybe that's why I didn't know right away you were one. I've never met an adult shifter who had never shifted before."

Penny wailed, "This is very weird!" and pulled the hood even farther up over her head, until she'd disappeared into it entirely.

Ashley sank down into the warm seat and sighed agreement, then crept her fingertips toward Penny, hoping to offer some comfort. After a few long seconds, Penny's own fingertips emerged and laced through Ashley's. A bubble of relief popped in Ashley's chest and she whispered, "It really is going to be okay, Penny. I'm sorry I freaked out. This didn't go how I imagined it would."

A thin giggle came from within the parka. "Imagine how I feel."

Ashley sat up again and carefully snaked her arm around Penny's shoulders, tugging her closer. The drummer slowly tipped over until she was pressed up against Ashley's side, completely hidden within the winter gear. Ashley, softly, said, "I'm not sure I *can* imagine how you feel. Which is why me freaking out was really not helpful."

Penny whispered, "Tell me about shifters," from within her bundle of winter clothes, and Ashley smiled, pressing her mouth against the parka's hood.

"We've been around for a long time. As long as true humans, probably. Maybe longer. I don't know. There aren't that many of us, but at the same time, there are a lot more than you'd think. Renaissance is a shifter town, which just means there are a lot of us who have settled here. You've never had any kind of major injury or anything, have you?"

Penny made a surprised sound and shook her head, just a rustle of movement. Ashley nodded. "I didn't think so, because we almost always instinctively shift to help ourselves heal. And if you've ever had blood drawn…do you have a rare blood type?"

For a moment, the drummer emerged from the parka, eyes large with surprise. "Yeah. How did you know?"

"Shifters usually do. I'm not sure if we've all got the same rare blood type or if it's something that shows up in true humans, too, but we're careful about getting our blood drawn, or having surgery. Mostly we're just people, Penny. It's just we can also turn into animals. And I don't know why you didn't know you couldn't. Your parents can't?"

"I was adopted," Penny said after a moment. "And I remember…I can hear it now." She sounded sad. "This dumb little voice in my head. It used to drive me nuts when I was eleven or twelve and I just wanted it to go away because I was afraid I was actually crazy. It finally did and I forgot about it, but I can hear it again now."

"Oh, honey. You weren't crazy. That's your partridge talking to you."

Penny sat up and pushed her hood back so she could give Ashley a hard stare.

Ashley couldn't help blurting a giggle. "Okay, okay, yes, I hear how that sounded. But it's true. My bear talks to me all the time. So you were never crazy, sweetheart. I get why you must have thought you were, though. You must have an awful lot of willpower, to suppress it that thoroughly. But you don't have to anymore. Everything's going to be okay now. You're a shifter, not crazy."

"I don't know," Penny whispered. "I think I *might* be crazy. You can't hear this thing. It sounds like a lunatic."

CHAPTER 16

*T*he bear is going to eat us, the voice inside Penny's head said. *Except it's not because it's our mate and everything's okay but it's definitely going to eat us. We should hide. But not from the bear. This is a nice nest. We're safe in it. It's warm. Let's lay some eggs.*

If she wasn't crazy, Penny thought, then she was going to go crazy pretty soon. She honestly didn't know what was worse: turning into a partridge, or turning out of a partridge and being naked, or the little voice's conviction that something was going to eat them. Her. "Are my pronouns 'they/them' now?" she asked faintly.

Ashley chuckled, a warm and surprisingly comforting sound from someone who had turned into a gigantic grizzly bear and started Penny's apparent descent into madness. "I don't know what other people do. I think of myself as me, but if I think of me and my bear, it's 'us.'"

"It's separate from you?" Penny whispered.

"Nnnnooooo, but yes? It's a personality of its own. It's chiller than I am. But it's also part of me. When I'm human, it's part of me. When I'm a bear, I'm part of it. If I don't have anything else to do besides bear, it's pretty easy to just bumble along and not worry about anything, but I can still think and plan like a human if I need to."

Penny, remembering the absolute brainless panic of being a partridge, shook her head. "I don't think I can think and plan as a...bird." That sounded ridiculous. "I couldn't even bring my clothes with me."

"You can," Ashley said encouragingly. "It'll just take some practice. I've been doing this my whole life. You just shifted for the very first time."

Clothes are like feathers, the partridge announced. *We're naked without them.*

"No shit!" Penny froze as the words burst out, then whispered, "You, uh. How do you talk to your bear? You can't talk aloud, right? Or people would think you were nuts."

"I think we all talk to them out loud sometimes, but no, you can talk to your partridge in your head." Ashley was obviously trying to sound calm and reasonable, but the words she was using, in the order she was using them in, were just absurd. "Look, Penny, I know you've got a hotel room, but I think maybe I should bring you back to my apartment tonight. You've had kind of a shock—"

The goddamn partridge in Penny's mind lit up like a cartoon bird zotted by an electric shock, all buzzy bolts and feathers outlined in blue. *WE'VE BEEN SHOCKED?!?!*

Penny said, "Oh my God," out loud. "Not that kind of shock." Although she felt a little like the aftermath of that kind of shock, all frazzled and like her hair was standing on end. "How do I make it shut up?"

"Your partridge?" Ashley hesitated. "I don't know if you can. I ignore my bear and sometimes she gives up, but you can't really make it be quiet, I don't think."

"Drumming," Penny said with sudden violence. "That's why I took up drumming. It drowned the damn thing out."

She sank back down into the fluffy coat, trying to hide from the world. Ashley, after another momentary pause, said, "Anyway, so I think maybe you shouldn't be alone tonight, and being around another shifter might help."

Not just another shifter, the partridge announced as if it was revealing something earth-shaking. *Our* **mate***.*

"Our mate," Penny echoed.

That, at least, felt right. It felt like something she'd known in her bones but hadn't quite been able to believe. Because who could believe it? Love at first sight wasn't something that happened, or at least, not often. Everybody knew somebody, of course. Somebody who had known right away, when they'd met the person they were going to marry. But that was the stuff of fairy tales, even if it did happen once in a while in real life.

Of course, turning into bears was also literally the stuff of fairy tales.

Turning into a partridge, not so much. "*Swans*, yes," Penny blurted. "But who the hell turns into a partridge? Is it because of my last name?" she demanded. "Is it, what's it called? When your name defines your destiny? My parents are Rich and Mary Beth Partridge so I turn into one? Is that it?"

"I don't think so," Ashley said cautiously. "I think it's innate. Someone in your birth family, somewhere along the line, was a shifter. Probably a partridge shifter, although there are unexpected mutations, sometimes. I know someone who's a giraffe. Just, like, randomly. The rest of his family are red pandas."

Penny's growing distress was temporarily derailed by that, turning into a helpless giggle. "That must have been a shock."

The partridge went *BZOT* blue in her head again.

Penny had been a shifter for about nine minutes, and she was going to kill the bird in her brain before she reached the tenth minute.

"It was," Ashley was saying with a smile. "The whole family ended up moving to Ireland when he was about six, to work and live at some wildlife park there where he could shift some of the time without drawing atten-tion. Red pandas can sneak around a town like Renais-sance pretty easily, but a giraffe stands out. So can I take you home? To my place?"

"Yeah," Penny whispered. "I think you're right, I probably shouldn't be alone. I feel like I'm losing my mind. Honestly, a partridge?"

"There are a huge number of predator shifters," Ashley said as she crawled back into the driver's seat. "I've got a theory that it was a survival adaptation. But there's something to be said for 'small and hides easily,' too, so there *are* non-predator shifters."

"I like how you manage not to say 'prey species' there."

Ashley grimaced into the rear-view mirror. "Shifters don't hunt other shifters so the whole idea gives me the creeps. I definitely don't think of non-predator shifters as prey species. Do you know anything about your birth parents?"

Penny turned her head to look out the window as they left the parking lot. "Nothing. It was a closed adoption and my birth mother didn't even leave any permission to access medical records. She couldn't have known, could she? I mean, if you knew you were a shifter how could you adopt your kid out into a—what did you call regular people?"

"True humans."

"Yeah. A true human family without some kind of warning?"

"I don't know. Maybe she didn't feel like she had any choice."

"Maybe." Penny pressed her head against the window. The partridge said *cold!* and she muttered, *I wouldn't be so cold if I'd stayed dressed when I shifted,* back at it.

The partridge gave an injured sniff. *The window is cold.*

Oh. Sorry. Oh, God, she was talking to the voice in her head. This couldn't possibly end well. "It doesn't matter," she said out loud. "I mean, obviously I want to know, but I accepted a long time ago that there were things I'd never know. This is much, much, much," she took a breath, "*much* weirder than the rest of it, but it's still the same kind of thing."

Ashley, quietly, said, "I'm here for you to talk to, if it helps."

"Right. My mate." That came out sharper than Penny meant it to, and she tried to soften her voice. "No, I mean it. My mate. I can feel it now. Or what I was feeling makes sense? It's this certainty, right here." She pressed the heel of her hand over her heart. "I just *know,* when I look at you. It's actually amazing, and if I wasn't completely freaked out I'd really be enjoying it. I'm sorry to take that away from you."

"You're not." Ashley flashed her a smile in the rear-view mirror. "Everybody says the first little while after you tell your mate about what you really are is weird. We have an extra helping of weird, that's all. I still know in my heart that I'm meant for you, and it's kind of amazing to hear that you know it in the same way now too. Fated mates are supposed to, but…it's different with two shifters, I think."

"Well, an hour ago I had a huge dumb crush and

ridiculous plans for a lifetime together even though we've only really known each other a few days across a couple of months. Now I've got a bird in my head telling me it wasn't a dumb crush, it was fate striking like a gong. I feel confident about it in a way I didn't. Even if I've got a talking bird in my head. Oh my god, I'm going insane."

Ashley laughed. "No, you're not. It'll be okay. Honestly, all I can think is you've got the world's strongest willpower and you just squished the partridge down because let's be real, who turns into a partridge? Or anything else, for that matter? But I'm going to get hold of Maggie flipping Ross and have her come over and explain how the hell she knew you were a shifter, and whether she's got any advice for a bird shifter, okay? I'm sure she and Conri are still in town. They can come over tomorrow."

"Yes," Penny said. "Because expecting world-famous professional wrestlers to just drop by and explain everything is perfectly normal."

"Okay, normally I would agree, but in this particular case I think I'm right." Ashley drove them up to a low, attractive apartment complex and came to open the car door for Penny.

The wall is falling! Help! Help! The wall is falling!

Penny froze with one foot out the door. *The 'wall' is a door and it **opened**. How can you know what a window is and not what a door is?*

The partridge also froze, everything motionless except its eyes, which darted around like it thought the question might be a trick. A longish silence suggested it wasn't going to answer, so Penny sighed and got out of the car. "If I go have a long sleep, everything will be normal in the morning, right?"

"For some value of normal?" Ashley suggested hopefully. "A new normal, one might say?"

Penny groaned. "Nobody likes that phrase."

"Yeah? Not even when your new normal is being a bonafide rock star?"

"That's different!"

The partridge thrust an image of shining, glittering rocks into Penny's mind. She stared at them—and staring at the inside of her head was an Experience—and then groaned. "No. Not shiny, starry rocks. Rock star."

She had never had the sensation of complete, befuddled blankness filling her skull before. There was a vast, echoing emptiness in which the idea of 'rock star' bounced around and found nothing to connect to. Having found nothing, the concept simply faded out of the partridge's mind entirely, incomprehensible and therefore apparently unworthy of any further contemplation.

Penny, quite clearly, and without all that much to attach it to yet either, thought, *Oh, no.* Unlike the partridge's dismissal of rock stars, though, that little 'oh no' lodged itself in the side of her mind, waiting for more things to stick itself to.

Ashley was smiling at her. "You're getting used to hearing it."

"I really don't think I am," Penny said dubiously. "But Im going to have to, aren't I?"

"I think it'll be easier after you've had some rest," Ashley murmured. "Come on upstairs. I'll make up the guest bed for you. Yes, the guest bed," she added firmly. "You need sleep and some time to adjust."

Penny wanted to protest, but the truth was, Ashley was right, and she was unconscious the minute she hit the pillows.

"PENNY?" A gentle tapping at the door and Ashley's cautious voice woke her in the morning. She had a moment of disorientation, not helped by the partridge yodeling *ARE WE LOST?!?!?!?!* inside her skull, before she remembered where she was and—belatedly, despite the birdbrain yelling in her head—what had happened.

She groaned. "Not dead. I think."

"Can I come in? I have coffee."

"Oh, bless you." Penny sat up blearily, scrubbing her hands over her face and tugging the oversized t-shirt she'd borrowed to sleep in up to cover her shoulder. "Yeah, come in."

Ashley came in wearing a snuggly-looking sweatshirt over jeans and bunny slippers. She handed Penny a large mug of coffee, and stood awkwardly while Penny slurped down the first sips before gesturing to the bed. "Go ahead, sit. It's your bed."

"But you're using it." Ashley smiled as she sat,

though, and tucked her hair up into some kind of twist that looked adorable and exactly perfect for a sleepy morning.

Although she seemed suspiciously bright-eyed and perky, now that Penny was awake enough to really look at her. "What time is it?"

"Eleven thirty. I've been up for a couple of hours. Maggie and Conri are going to stop by around one. I thought we might try—"

A hopeful flush of heat rushed through Penny and was squashed when Ashley went on with "—practicing shifting with your clothes. I tried forgetting my clothes and getting them back this morning, a few times. I lost one pair of pyjamas and a slipper," she said, lifting her foot to look sadly at the bunnies, "but the second time it worked, so I think I can talk you through it."

"You only lost one slipper?"

"One of them came back the first time I tried to fetch them. It was my favorite," she said, still sort of sadly.

"You have a single favorite slipper…?"

"I'm sure that's perfectly normal," Ashley said with a sniff.

Penny laughed and drank enough coffee that she wasn't in danger of spilling any when she leaned over a bit to bump her shoulder against Ashley's. "It is. Totes normal. Okay, yes," she said more hesitantly. "I think we should try the clothes thing. I'd really like to get that dress back if I can."

"Right." Ashley pressed her lips together. "The thing is, um. I think you're going to have to start naked."

Penny's eyebrows shot up. "I like how this conversation is going."

Ashley blushed and put her face in her hands. Muffled, she said, "Not that I object to that direction, but it's not what I meant. If you shift while wearing clothes, then the ones that will most naturally come back with you are the ones you were wearing when you shifted. So if you want to try to retrieve that dress…"

Penny giggled, caught a glimpse of Ashley's blushing cheeks, and giggled again. "Right. Okay. So talk me through it while I finish this cup of genuinely very excellent coffee?"

Ashley lifted her head, still pink of cheek. "I've been thinking about it all morning. It's hard to even figure out, because I've been doing it since before I can remember, but I think basically what happens is I think of my clothes as part of myself. They're not, obviously, but for shifting purposes, they kind of are."

Like feathers! the partridge said with enthusiasm. *If we shifted without our feathers we'd be NAKED.* It provided an image of a plucked chicken. Or, Penny guessed, a plucked partridge. They looked a lot alike. Aloud, with a grimace, she said, "Like feathers. Or fur."

"Exactly. Although if we shift naked we aren't furless when we shift, but never mind that, that complicates things. So…" Ashley held her breath. "So really I think you should probably just try shifting naked a few times to get used to what it feels like. You were pretty freaked out last night. With justification!" she said as Penny bugged her eyes at her. "But I think getting a little bit used to what it feels like will help when you try to bring your clothes back."

"Okay, yeah, no, that makes sense. Okay, fine. Starkers it is."

CHAPTER 17

*P*enny, with absolutely no visible sign of self-consciousness, simply stood up and stripped her sleeping shirt off. Ashley yelped and turned away, blushing and crushing her eyes shut, and heard the amusement in Penny's voice. "Does the sight of me naked offend you so much?"

"I just don't want to be rude! Or…rude!" There were quite a few other words that actually leaped to mind there, but Ashley didn't think discussing how hot and bothered she got looking over Penny's lush curves would help at all just then.

"Well, I feel silly standing here naked with your back to me. Believe me, people spend a lot of time undressed, or half dressed, backstage at concert venues, so it doesn't bother me at all. Seriously, Ashley, how do I do this? I don't even know how to shift. It happened accidentally last night. My partridge went 'I can do that!' and just, like, *did*."

Ashley kept her gaze resolutely on the floor. "Ask it if it can do that again."

There was the briefest pause and then a telltale rush of air, followed by a startled squawk. Ashley twisted to find a wide-eyed partridge standing on the floor, braced like it was expecting something to go wrong.

She was a rather pretty bird, all dusky browns with white and reddish-brown highlights on her wings. Her neck was speckled with black, her throat cream, and her beak, eye rings, and legs were all a splendid red. She was, Ashley suspected, probably twice the size of a true partridge: shifter animals were almost always larger than their true counterparts, and Ashley had the vague idea that normal partridges were smaller than an average chicken. Penny was definitely bigger than that, particularly with her feathers fluffed in alarm, as they currently were.

"That's good," Ashley crooned. She didn't think of herself as a crooner, but it was the only appropriate tone to take with a nervous bird. "That's very good. Now can you shift back?"

The partridge stared at her suspiciously, then marched around in a little circle as if it was thinking very hard. Another *bamf* of air puffed, and all at once Penny was standing there again, her bare back to Ashley.

She had, Ashley thought, an *awfully* cute bottom.

"That," Penny breathed, "is freaky. Let me try again." She shifted again, still strutting in a little circle, although she froze once more when she did shift, as if she'd surprised herself and had forgotten how to walk. Then, cautiously, she walked around some more, shifting a couple more times before hunkering down in partridge form and, Ashley swore, concentrating fiercely. She wondered if *she* looked like that when she concentrated as a bear. It was ridiculously cute, honestly. Animals weren't really suppose to concentrate, and the result was adorable.

Penny sat there with that intense partridgey frown for long enough that Ashley wondered if she should say or do something, but very suddenly the partridge shifted back to a woman again, and this time, she was dressed. Mostly, at least: she was in the gorgeous autumnal concoction she'd rented, although her legs and feet were bare. She looked down at herself, yelped, "Oh thank God!" and collapsed over backward on the bed in a rustle of skirts. "Oh my god, that was the hardest thing I've ever done in my life. Do you *know* how hard it is to get a partridge to focus on a dress? *Yes* it's like feathers!" she wailed in despair, clearly to the partridge, then said to Ashley, "It got so hung up on the idea of feathers it wouldn't shift because humans don't have feathers. Oh my *God.* Is your bear that..." She sputtered out, giving up, then exhaled more quietly and ran her hands over the dress. "At least I got it back."

"That's wonderful." Ashley beamed at her. "Really, I'm very proud of you. That was hard and you did a great job!"

"Thank you. Can I borrow some giant-sized clothes

that don't matter if I lose them in a shift? I mean, it would matter, obviously, but—"

Ashley grinned. "But it wouldn't be a holy-cow-*how-much?* dress if they disappear. Yeah, of course. I have a couple of skirts that might fit you, and my shirts will be too big, but that's a look, right?"

"The skirts had better be mini, or I'll be walking on the hems. Yes, that would be great, please. Oh!" She sat up and looked down the dress, then collapsed again in relief. "Oh, good, my bra came back with the dress. I wish the shoes had, but I can borrow those big snow boots again, at least long enough to get back to the hotel."

Ashley, genuinely curious, said, "You couldn't tell your bra had come back?"

Penny waved a hand in the air. "This dress has a lot of structural boning. It was fifty-fifty on the bra."

Ashley laughed. "Right, of course. Yeah, let me get you the clothes, and then if you're hungry I'll find something for breakfast. Which means we'll probably eat gingerbread man cookies because that's what I've got in the kitchen right now."

"Not a cook?" Penny sat up again, interested, and Ashley answered as she left the room to find Penny some clothes.

"Not really, no? There's never seemed like much point in cooking for one, and even before I was running the pub I was always pretty busy. I'm capable of producing something edible in a kitchen, but only under duress. You?"

"I make two kinds of food," Penny called, though she lowered her voice as Ashley came back in with a skirt and top. "One: massive party feasts for fifty. Two: peanut butter and jelly sandwiches. Oh, that's cute. And it is a miniskirt. On you." She held up a denim skirt that was short on Ashley, then stepped into it, displaying how it hit her nicely at mid-thigh. "Amazingly, it fits around the waist, though. I'm now envisioning a future where I can borrow all of my girlfriend's clothes. Unzip me?" She turned to display the complicated zip-and-hook closure of her fairy gown, and Ashley found her hands cold and shaking with nerves as she tried to open it.

Penny glanced over her shoulder, a smile sparkling in her brown eyes. "Is this going to be a problem when we get to unfastening bras?"

"I will never master undoing them with one hand," Ashley whispered, mortified.

Penny laughed. "Me either, honestly. It's witchcraft. Ooh, I can breathe now, thanks." She took a deep breath and shimmied out of the dress, picking it up to lay it on the bed before pulling Ashley's shirt on.

It was slightly longer than the skirt on her. They both looked at where the hem skimmed just above her knees before Penny giggled and tucked it in. "I could have just borrowed this and a belt and I would've been fine. Okay, I'm ready for gingerbread men."

"I can probably do a *little* better than that," Ashley said guiltily.

"You say that like I'm not happy to eat gingerbread

for breakfast." Penny followed Ashley out of the bedroom, glancing around the two-bedroom apartment's open-plan layout. "This is nice. Big living room. Enough space to be a bear?"

"Especially if I push the coffee table out of the way." Ashley had, in fact, done that so she could shift back and forth as she experimented with her clothes. "Gingerbread is good, but shifting takes energy, especially when you're not used to it. Eggs and toast. Maybe bacon if I've got some in the freezer." She went to poke around, emerged triumphant, and got everything going in the small kitchen. Penny checked the fridge, found orange juice, and poured them both glasses, then sat at the kitchen bar to watch Ashley cook, and to consider the question when Ashley asked, "So how are you doing with all of this?"

"I don't know," Penny confessed. "Okay? Maybe? I guess? It's weird and I don't feel like it suddenly fills some kind of 'my god, I always knew there was something missing' space in my life. But it's also fine? It would be finer if this damn bird would stop…I think it forgets how to swallow if it pauses taking a drink, you know? But it's okay. I do think part of the reason I started playing drums was to drown it out, so it's nice to know I wasn't crazy."

"I think you're handling it really well, for what it's worth. And I'm really impressed you were able to get the dress back. I hope Maggie will be able to answer some of your questions." Ashley gave Penny a shy smile. "And I hope you might think about telling my family about all this sometime, too. It doesn't have to be right away, but..."

"But you want to be able to tell them you met your mate," Penny guessed. "That's got to be a big deal for shifters. I mean, real ones like you. Not that I'm not a real shifter, I guess, but you know what I mean!"

"It is a big deal for those of us who grew up knowing it was a possibility, yeah. But," Ashley emphasized, "I *also* know I have like eleven million cousins and they're all huge and overwhelming and if you want to wait three *years* I'll understand that, too!"

Penny laughed. "Maybe three days, at least, while I get my feet under me. My...claws? Talons? I guess I mostly think of bird feet as 'feet,' though. That smells delicious," she added as her stomach growled audibly. "Am I allowed to eat like four eggs? And also is it cannibalism if I eat eggs now?"

Ashley's mouth fell open as she contemplated that question. "I never thought about it before. I don't think so? Maybe avoid partridge eggs, though."

"I've managed to do that so far in my life, so it shouldn't be too hard to keep on keeping on." Penny accepted a large plate of scrambled eggs and bacon, humming happily as she ate. "Those are really good scrambled eggs. They've got some kind of little twist to them I've never tasted before."

"I put Worcestershire sauce in them. Just a splash. A family friend did that once when I was over for breakfast and I loved it so I've always made them that way."

"No way. It's really good!"

"Thanks."

They lingered over breakfast, then hopped up guiltily when a knock sounded at the door, like they should have been doing—Ashley didn't know what, but apparently not giggling over toast crusts. Maggie Ross and Conri Lyell were at the door, as expected, and Ashley invited them in, slightly stunned at the wrestler's height. She'd been tall the night before, obviously, but Ashley had been in shoes then, and now with Maggie in heels and Ashley in bunny slippers, the athlete was about six inches taller than herself.

We could still swat her, her bear said consolingly.

The idea nearly made Ashley laugh, so she was smiling as she said, "Hey, hi, thank you for coming, I really appreciate it. Come in, please! You remember Penny?"

"Of course." Maggie spoke for the two of them, though Conri smiled and nodded as they came in. Penny stood up to greet them, and looked unbelievably tiny next to the tall wrestler. Even Conri, who was probably five ten, looked whip-slender and like a breeze would knock him over, beside Maggie. They were an interesting couple, with her tremendous pale height and his sallower wolfishness, and it was highlighted even more by Maggie's flowing hippie dress and coat compared to Conri's incredibly well-cut business suit. The only thing they obviously had in common was a fondness for long hair: Conri's was pulled back in a thin ponytail, and Maggie's thick white braid fell down her spine like a rope.

She looked absolutely delighted as she sat down across from Penny. "You figured it out. I can sense you now."

"You could before," Ashley said. "*How?* Can I get you some coffee? Water?"

"Coffee," Conri said. "Please. Can I help?"

Ashley smiled and shook her head. "No, the kitchen's only big enough for one. Thanks, though. Please, have a seat." She went into the kitchen with her bear craning its head toward Conri curiously.

We could swat him, but he is...strong, the bear said after a moment. *For a wolf, he is **very** strong.*

Ashley shrugged. *I suppose some must be.*

I don't like it, the bear announced. *It makes my fur itch.*

Well, he won't be here long, Ashley promised.

Maggie was saying, "I couldn't sense it, exactly, but I could see you were a bird shifter. It's something about the bone structure, or the eyes, or something. I don't know. I could tell you didn't know it, though, or that you rarely shifted."

"I didn't know," Penny confirmed. "Until last night when Ashley showed me her bear and I shifted. She says that's really unusual, that I must be very strong-willed to have suppressed it. Do you know anybody else like me?"

Ashley looked over her shoulder to see Maggie and Conri exchanging glances. "No," Conri said after a moment. "I know that in our shifter line, there are people who could force a shifter to shift, or not to. But

I've never met anybody who suppressed it themselves, besides you."

Penny said, "*Your* shifter line?" at the same time Ashley's bear said, *People like **him***, with a growl. Ashley, without meaning to, said, "People like you?" out loud, and got a startled look from both the wolf shifter and the big swan at his side.

Conri, reluctantly, said, "Yes. It's a power in my family line. I foreswore it, but yes. I could force someone in our line to shift, or not," to all of them, and then to Penny, "Shifters come from all kinds of different provenances. Maggie's and my line might be the newest, the only one that really knows where it started. It began in the Roman arenas. But we developed all over the world, so we have to have come from different beginnings."

"Hnh. That makes sense. But you don't know anybody else like me. Oh my God!" Penny straightened. "Does that mean I'm a different kind of shifter than the rest of you? Because I *could* suppress it?"

"I suppose it's possible," Conri said, startled. "I have no idea if that's a thing."

Maggie said, "Joash would know," and her husband gave her a flat look as Ashley brought coffee over and sat beside Penny.

"I'm not flying Joash all the way from Italy to answer questions, Maggie."

"While I agree Joash would be happiest to be flown around the world for a conversation, there are these things called telephones these days, you know. I hear they work all over the whole world, even."

"It's—" Conri broke off, his mouth working with irritation before he muttered, "It's six or seven in the evening there, isn't it. I got my time zones mixed up for a minute and was going to say it was five in the morning. He'd be asleep."

"He's a cat," Maggie said. "He could be asleep at literally any time. Go on, give him a call. If anybody knows, he will."

"Why?" Ashley asked. "Who is he?"

"A big, pretty, lazy lunk," Maggie replied with a grin. "But he knows everything there is to know about shifters, so if the ability to suppress *being* a shifter is a thing, he'll be the man to tell us."

"Fine," Conri said with a roll of his eyes. He already had his phone out, and turned it to show them the video call he was putting through. "We'll ask him your questions."

The call went through faster than Conri Lyell expected, because a video image flashed on before he could turn the phone back to himself. Penny nearly laughed: Maggie was right. Well, she couldn't tell if this Joash person was lazy or big, but he was *certainly* pretty, even through a six inch video screen. He had dark auburn hair and nearly golden eyes, and skin that looked like he'd been sun-bronzed by an expert. She said, "You really *are* pretty," with her outside voice, and couldn't even be mortified about it, although her partridge rolled its eyes up and collapsed in a dead faint. Ashley, at Penny's side, gave a staccato laugh.

"And you," the man on the phone said, "are a Sixty Pix. Penny, the drummer, am I correct? It's a pleasure and a delight to meet you."

"Holy shit. I can't—yes, but how did you know that?"

"Your band is taking the world by storm, my dear, and I do like to keep abreast of these things. But I must ask: have you kidnapped Conri Lyell and are using his phone to call me for ransom? I assure you I have no intention of paying it. I can give you his bank account numbers, though, and you can feel free to help yourself."

"How the hell do you have my bank account numbers?" Conri turned the phone back to face himself, and the man on the phone's rich laughter drifted out.

"There you are. Don't ask questions you don't want answers to, Conri. It's lovely to see you."

Conri mumbled something, then more clearly, said, "We have a question we do want an answer to, though. Penny's just discovered she's a shifter."

"At her tender age? Do turn the phone around again, Conri, I've seen your narrow face many times and suspect I'll have very few opportunities to rest my eyes on the visual feast of the young women you're visiting. Maggie, if you'd like to move over there with the other women, I would enjoy that very much."

Maggie laughed. "You see me plenty, Joash. This is Ashley Torben. She lives here in Renaissance."

"I assure you that as magnificent as the Renaissance was, no one in the modern world wishes to return to that misbegotten era. Ah, thank you, Conri." Joash, facing them again, winked, then studied Penny thoughtfully. "A new shifter? In your thirties? Unusual, but not entirely unheard of."

"Does it mean I'm part of a particular shifter line?" Penny asked eagerly. It would be a kind of an answer about some of her history, shifter or not, and she would like that.

"I'm afraid it's more typically a self-preservation technique. There are shifters with long lives, but they don't normally begin shifting late. They just live a long time. But if you've been raised by true humans and have no hint of your heritage, suppressing the shift can keep you safe. If you were raised by shifters—"

Penny shook her head, and the red-haired man nodded sympathetically. "Almost certainly self-preservation, then. That, and extraordinary willpower. Shifting is a base instinct for us. Most of the shifters I know who were raised by true humans still began to shift when they hit their teen years. You must be very stubborn."

"I guess I am." Penny sagged a little. "I guess I was also hoping I might get an answer that cleared up my entire life. Not that I had all that many questions about it before I turned out to be a magical non-human being."

Joash chuckled, a warm and inviting sound. "I'm afraid I can't provide the answers to life, the universe, and everything, but I do have some friends who could look into your background for you, if you wanted. People with considerable expertise in researching those of us with more unusual family lines, shall we say."

"Oh." Penny held her breath, then bit the inside of her lip. "Can I think about that a little bit?"

"Of course. Conri will provide you with my contact details. Feel free to reach out at any time, and if you're in Italy, do drop by for a visit. Bring the rest of your band. I'm sure we can arrange a little venue for you to play. The Colosseum, perhaps."

He hung up while Penny was still trying to collect her jaw. "The *Colosseum*? *The* Colosseum? He's not serious, is he?"

"Rarely," Maggie said dryly. "But he also probably means it. If I were you I'd write a song for your band that really wants a video shot at the Colosseum. Joash will make it happen."

"How?" Penny's voice rose. "Who *is* he?"

"He's very rich, very charming, and very well-connected," Conri said in much the same tone Maggie had used. "I'm sorry he couldn't give you any more concrete answers, Penny, but it's not an entirely bad thing to be told you have epic willpower, is it?"

Penny ducked her head. "No, I guess not. And it's probably better to have been safe than sorry. I'm not sure my parents would have reacted all that well to watching me turn into a partridge over dinner."

The partridge, rousing from its faint, sent an image of flapping wildly over mashed potatoes. Penny sent a picture of herself eating a nice chicken and gravy dinner to go with the mashed potatoes.

The partridge fainted again.

"I'm glad you found yourself," Maggie said as Penny

bit back a laugh at the partridge. "I'm also glad Ashley invited us over, because I was going to have to invite myself otherwise. There's something you should know about bird shifters."

"Oh?" Penny straightened, suddenly nervous.

"Shifters tend to be big, you know that?"

Penny shook her head, and Maggie paused, recalibrating. "Well, we do. Bigger than our true counterparts. I'm not sure why, when it comes to bears and wolves and other big ones, but it makes sense for birds. That's a lot of mass to shift."

Conri blew air through his nose and muttered, "Magic. That's why we're bigger."

Maggie rolled her eyes. "Yeah, I know, Con, but it still doesn't make sense. Anyway, wolves and bears and things, they can't change their size. Conri's massive, but he's—well, show her, Conri."

Penny said, "Change their size?" under the rest of what Maggie said. Conri gave his partner a fondly exasperated look and rose, shaking himself loosely and then shifting.

The goddamn partridge woke up long enough to shriek *OH MY GOD IT'S A WOLF* and then passed out again as Penny gaped at what was, indeed, a wolf. The biggest wolf she could possibly imagine. Rangy and slender, not unlike Conri himself, but it turned out *rangy and slender* on a wolf that stood as tall as she did was actually *fricking massive*. He had a huge grey ruff, and enormously large golden eyes to go along with appallingly big teeth and claws. Penny squeaked, and

Conri shifted back to human, looking decidedly more wolfish around the edges than he had before. At least to her mind.

"So," Maggie said cheerfully, "that's as big or as small as he gets. Big, very big, but that's it. I, on the other hand—"

"I saw you last night," Penny said. "You were as tall as he is. As a wolf, I mean. I mean, you as a swan were as big as he is as a wolf. Oh, God, I sound like I'm losing my mind."

"I was showing off," Maggie said with a lazy grin. "I could have been smaller. Here." She didn't bother standing up. She just shifted, and there was abruptly a swan on the couch.

Swans were not small birds, but this one wasn't as freakishly large as the one who'd been at the charity venue the night before. It was big. Bigger than Penny thought of swans as being, even if she knew they were big. But not *that* big. The swan transformed back to Maggie, who kept talking like she hadn't just taken a moment to be a bird. "That's my smallest size. Maybe a third larger than a regular swan."

"Wait, your smallest size?" Penny's head was spinning, although the partridge, thank god, was still unconscious, and had no opinions to offer. "I thought you just said shifters only…but you were smaller, so…" She stared at Maggie a few seconds. "So what's your biggest size?"

This time Maggie stood up and stepped away from the couch, eyeing the living room cautiously. "This is going to be a little overwhelming. You all might want to…"

"Move the furniture," Conri said dryly. "You can help, Maggie. You're the strongest of us."

Ashley made a sound of protest that caused Maggie to flash a grin at her. "Yeah, I know, bear. You're probably at least as strong as I am in human form and we all know you're much stronger in bear form, but—"

"Wait, you're extra strong?" Penny turned to Ashley, distracted and a bit fluttery. The wretched partridge woke up enough to flutter, too. Fluttery wings, fluttery eyelashes. Not that birds were known for their eyelashes, but it was certainly *trying* to flutter them. Penny ignored it, or at least tried to, because the idea of Ashley being very, *very* strong was for some reason extremely hot. She wet her lips and swallowed, and Ashley gave her a long, slow grin.

"I'm pretty strong, yeah. We can talk about it later."

A tiny girlish giggle burst from Penny's throat and she was absolutely certain she was blushing as the other two shifters in the room laughed.

"—*but*," Maggie said loudly, "for the purposes of moving furniture, let's assume I'm going to be more helpful than Penny. Conri's right, we should move it. I'll put it back," she promised, and then with the effortlessness of long practice and great strength, she and Ashley picked up first the couch, then the other seating, and moved them to clear the floor as much as possible. Maggie put the coffee table *on* the couch, then sat down in the middle of the empty floor. "This is

going to be startling," she repeated. "You should probably back up."

Penny, mystified, got about halfway through saying,
"How big are you going to *get*?" when Maggie shifted
and answered that question.

Immensely, enormously *huge*, that was how big.
Even sitting, even with her long neck curled down and
her wings tucked in and her feet not visible under a
truly incredible amount of white feathers, Maggie the
swan, at her largest size, quite literally filled the room.
There was clearance between the top of her back and
the ceiling, but only just, and none of them, not even
Conri, had stepped far enough back. The sheer size of
the swan pushed them farther away, faces full of
feathers.

Penny's partridge shrieked, *BIG! I CAN DO THAT!*
and, to Penny's horror, shifted.

There was absolutely no room in the apartment for
one, much less two, ginormous birds. Maggie shifted
back to human instantly, while Penny gave a
triumphant *ka-chu-CHU!* call.

She was so big. She didn't fit in the apartment,
either, not if she stood up. She hunched down, sitting
on her feet but perking her head up, looking around,
and bumped her head on the ceiling. The partridge
shrieked *ATTACKED!* and flung its wings open, trying
to make Penny bigger.

No! We're big enough already! And knocking things
off Ashley's walls, and knocking people over, and all
sorts of terrible chaotic things. Penny pulled her wings

back in, trying to shift back to human, but the partridge was hopping around, whacking its head on the ceiling and bumping back down to the floor, shouting *ka-chu, ka-chu-chu!* in a panic. Penny could hardly imagine what her claws were doing to the carpet. Bad things. Very bad things. *CALM DOWN!*

Because yelling 'calm down' at anything was, historically, an enormously successful way to get things to calm down. Penny hopped around the apartment even faster, wrecking everything she came into contact with, until suddenly Ashley was right in front of her, murmuring, "It's okay. It's okay, baby. I know, you're awfully big, aren't you? It's scary. But it's all right. Nothing here will hurt you. You know me, right? It's Ashley, your mate. Remember me, sweetheart? Yeah, it's okay."

The smooth gentle cadence of her voice sounded so much like a mother hen crooning over her chicks that the partridge's feathers began to settle. Penny turned her head, looking at Ashley from first one eye, then the other. She was very small. That was funny: Ashley was anything but small. But right now she was. Penny had to be at least eight feet tall, herself. More than that, because the ceiling was probably eight feet and her back was pressed up against it when she straightened her legs.

A thought trickled through the partridge's mind: maybe squishing up against the ceiling wasn't necessary. With some effort, it settled down, looking at Ashley from an equal height now. She still looked quite small, her entire head smaller than Penny's beak, but she smiled. "Good job, that's good, sweetheart. See, you're nice and safe. Do you think you can shift back now?"

With a *thump*, Penny shifted back to human. It was *cold* in the apartment with no feathers, and she shivered violently as Conri squeaked and spun around, putting his back to her. Ashley, hardly missing a beat, snatched a blanket off the back of the couch and draped it around Penny, and only as it settled on her bare skin did Penny realize she'd forgotten her clothes. "Oh *no!*"

"It happens to the best of us," Maggie said through a grin. "Usually when we're intoxicated, but it happens. I didn't expect you to go big right away!"

"The damn partridge thought 'I can do that!' and did," Penny said miserably. "I hope I didn't hurt anything."

"Nothing that can't be fixed easily." Ashley hugged her. "Why don't you go get dressed while we put the furniture back, and then if you have any other questions maybe Maggie can answer them."

Instead of going to get dressed, Penny looked pathetically at the swan shifter. "How big were we?"

"As far as I can tell, the biggest we get is about fourteen feet at the shoulder. With my neck I'm, I don't know, twenty, twenty-two feet tall at the tip of my bill, if I'm stretching? You're probably only seventeen feet or so, all stretched out. Maybe not quite. But still, huge."

"Birds that big can't fly, can they?" Penny asked, incredulous.

"True birds, no, but we've got magic to help. Otherwise we'd just be dinosaurs."

Penny stared at her. "Oh my God. Oh my *God*. Are there dinosaur shifters?"

"Not as far as I know," Maggie said cheerfully. "It's just us big birds out there representing for our lost ancestors. Go get dressed," she said more gently. "Conri and I have to head out, but now that you know you *can* shift big, that's the protection you need against not doing it accidentally."

"I just did it accidentally!"

"But you won't again," Maggie said with confidence, and Penny, with a despairing glance at Ashley, went to borrow more clothes.

CHAPTER 19

It took a few minutes to get the living room straightened out again. There were a number of extremely large feathers lying around. Ashley collected them, then, grinning, put them in a vase. No one would believe they were real, anyway. Penny emerged in a pair of Ashley's sweat pants and a t-shirt with an apologetic expression and examined the scratches she'd left in the floor before they said goodbye to Maggie and Conri.

Then Penny threw herself onto the couch and pulled a pillow over her head. "I'm a disaster."

Ashley crawled after her and tugged her into her arms for a hug. "You're not."

"No, honestly, I think I am. I can't control this thing at all. I scratched up your floor and left feathers every-where. It's a miracle I didn't poop all over everything."

Ashley, who hadn't considered that frightened birds did tend to loosen their bowels, struggled not to laugh, and ended up burying her face in Penny's shoulder, shaking with giggles. "It is a miracle. Oh, gosh. Thank you for not doing that. That would have been so very gross."

"See?" Penny wailed. "A disaster!"

"You've been a shifter for about..." Ashley twisted, looking for a clock, then gave up and guessed at it: "About twelve hours, Penny. I think you're entitled to a little bit of disaster."

"And I lost your clothes!"

"Well, you can always get naked and try to get them back." Heat flushed through Ashley and she laughed, quick and quiet and nervous. "Um, that sounded...not how I meant it to sound."

Penny craned her neck to smile up at Ashley, her brown eyes sparkling. "Does that mean we're not at the 'get naked' stage of our relationship? I have to say, as far as I can tell, we've always been at it. We just haven't been at the 'Ashley looks at naked Penny' part."

Ashley, face hotter than before, made a faint protest. "We haven't been at the 'Penny looks at naked Ashley' part either!"

"But that," Penny said wisely, "is a lack of opportunity, not a lack of scruples. You have scruples. You are scrupulous. I, on the other hand, am immoral and dishonorable and will happily look at beautiful naked women with only the slightest bit of encouragement. Sorry," she added more quietly. "I'm not really an asshole. Just a little on edge."

"You have every reason to be." Ashley smiled and

put her mouth against Penny's shoulder, then left a kiss in that spot. "I'd be lying if I said I wasn't also intrigued by the 'getting naked' prospect. I just don't want to take advantage of you in an altered state."

Penny laughed. "It would be hard for me to get in a more altered state than I've been since last night, it's true. Oh my God, what if I turned into a partridge while having sex?"

Ashley, fervently, said, "Please don't," and Penny laughed again.

"At this point I can't make any promises. Well, I suppose I could promise no hanky panky until I was sure of my shifting abilities?"

"Did you really just say hanky panky?"

"I did." Penny squirmed around in Ashley's arms until she was facing her, and smiling. "Is that a mood-killer?"

"Not nearly as much as turning into a partridge would be." Ashley leaned in to kiss her, soft and hopeful. Penny made a sweet sound and scooted a little closer, sliding her hands into Ashley's hair. Ashley groaned and pulled her all the way into her lap.

Penny yelped, but it was a delighted sound. "Is that some of that super-bear-strength? Probably not. I'm small and you're tall. You smell nice," she added in a murmur, nuzzling at Ashley's throat. "Sort of rich and musky. Not all frilly and floral like most women's toiletries. I smell frilly," she admitted.

"You smell delicious," Ashley murmured. Penny did smell frilly, in a way. Soft, like vanilla and oranges.

"And no, that's not bear-strong. I reserve that for when I know a girl likes to be pinned down."

Penny's eyes went huge. She raised both her hands above her head, wrists crossed, and heat crashed through Ashley so fast that she shivered. Penny's wrists were small, easy to wrap just one of her own hands around, and the sound Penny made in response was just *gorgeous*. Compliant and sweet, with just a murmur of shock. Ashley whispered, "Penny," and then let her wrists go, a little because she didn't trust herself, and more because she wanted to capture Penny's face in her hands and devour her with a kiss.

Her mouth was so sweet, warm and welcoming, and tasting a little of bacon, if Ashley was going to be honest. But then, she probably did too. She kissed Penny again, greedily, trying to take her breath and knowing she'd succeeded when Penny made the smallest whimper and melted against her. It took effort to break the kiss and to ask, right against Penny's mouth, "How far do you want this to go, Penny? Because I'm feeling a little all or nothing right now."

Penny whispered, "All. I'm always an all-in kind of girl. Oh my God, Ashley, you're *strong*."

Ashley grinned, still against her mouth. "You like it?"

"Not with guys." Penny sounded dizzy. "And honestly I'm usually the, uh, the pushy one with girls. I think I might like to be pushed a little, though. If it's you pushing."

"Tell me something else." Ashley pushed Penny's

chin up with her nose and found the tendon in her neck, nipping at it. "How do you feel about dirty talk?"

"Again, not so crazy about it with men, but..." Penny shivered all over, deliciously. "I think I'm willing to experiment?"

"Good, because I want to spread your legs and fuck you silly, baby. I want to listen to you beg me for more and come until you can't think, and to know I'm the one making you feel that way." While Penny gasped, Ashley pushed her t-shirt off, delighted to see Penny's bra was the same kind of all-lace one she'd spilled beer on months earlier. "God, that's pretty. You're pretty. C'mere, baby. I've got plans for you." She slid Penny's hands behind her back, catching her wrists in one hand again, and lowered her mouth to tease at a lace-covered nipple, gently at first and then with careful teeth and tongue, suckling it to an aching peak. Her free hand found Penny's other nipple, plucking and pulling at it until Penny was rolling her hips against Ashley's, whimpering breathlessly.

"Ash, Ashley, but I can't, I can't touch you when you have my hands, I want to touch you too?"

The words were almost a whine, exactly what Ashley wanted to hear, and she lifted a wicked smile at her mate, nuzzling at her mouth before saying, "No."

"But!" The little protest burst out and Ashley swallowed it with a kiss, pushing Penny backward against the couch cushions.

"No. No buts. You're mine right now. *God,* you're pretty. Look at those tits, Pen." Ashley brought her mouth back down to Penny's breasts, nibbling and sucking still through the bra, seeing what her mate liked and grinning when she earned particularly sharp gasps or moans. Penny was all curves and pale skin, although Ashley's view was badly interrupted by the borrowed sweatpants the other woman wore. "Gotta get rid of these. Might keep the panties on, though, if they match the bra. I love a woman in lingerie."

"Please," Penny whispered. "Please, Ashley. Please, I need you so bad it hurts, I'm aching, I'm so hot and wet." She almost faltered at the last words, but Ashley raised her head, smiling.

"Oh, that's good. That's good, Penny. Tell me every-thing, baby. I like it." She pushed the sweatpants down, glancing down the pale curves of Penny's body to discover her panties did, indeed, match the lacy bra. "Oh, perfect. Good girl. God, I've been waiting for you my whole life!" She slid her fingertips up Penny's thigh, very light touch to encourage her legs to open, and they did, as Penny whimpered again. "Good girl," Ashley murmured again. "I'm going to tease you now, baby. Just stroke you through the lace until you're desperate, how does that sound?"

"I'm already desperate!" Penny blurted.

Ashley laughed. "God, no, sweetheart, you're not. Come on, baby. Open. Open up." She traded her atten-tion back and forth between Penny's breasts as she stroked her, keeping her wrists held snugly at the small of her back, until Penny's hips were rising and falling and she was squirming, panting, obviously trying to get a firmer touch between her thighs. "You ready for me to fuck you, Penny?"

"*Please*! Oh my god, please, please!" Penny opened her legs farther and with a happy cackle, Ashley slid her fingers inside her panties, over a little thatch of curls to lodge her thumb against Penny's clit as her braided fingers slid inside her. Penny went rigid, crying out, so teased and ready that wet heat flooded over Ashley's hand almost instantly.

"Oh, good *girl*." Ashley covered Penny's mouth with her own, circling her clit and thrusting her fingers deeper inside her mate until Penny went rigid again, her cry swallowed by Ashley's kiss. "That's good, that's right, c'mon, baby, come for me again and then I'll let you rest. God, you're perfect. Fuck, I want you."

"Uh huh, please yes please oh god please?" Penny's voice rose, and rose again as Ashley found a perfect teasing circle to bring her up again with, until she was crying out loud with pleasure and then, reluctantly, overwhelmed, with, "Oh god no, I can't, I can't, too much too sensitive oh god enough enough?"

Ashley laughed softly and let her wrists go, pulling Penny across her lap to kiss her and cuddle her while she caught her breath. Penny was all softness and gasps against her, coming down from orgasm and finally, weakly, lifting her head to seek kisses. "Ashley." The name was soft and worshipful, the most wonderful sound Ashley had ever heard.

She murmured, "Penny," back, incredibly content.

"My mate. My beautiful woman, my god, you're gorgeous. And you didn't turn into a partridge."

Penny, taken completely by surprised, shouted with laughter, but before she could speak again, Ashley slid her hands into her hair and pulled her into a kiss. "Tell me something, baby." The kiss intensified, commanding Penny's attention until the other woman was half drunk on kisses before she turned a lustful, hopeful look into Ashley's gaze. "Tell me, baby. Do you go down?"

Penny's whimper came from the bottom of her soul as she slid off the couch to look up at Ashley worshipfully. Ashley's heart lurched, heat stinging between her thighs, and she stood right in front of Penny, so close the other woman should have leaned back to give her space. She didn't, though, and Ashley thought her knees would go weak from it as she pulled her own shirt off, lost her bra, then pushed her jeans and panties down. Penny whispered, "Oh my God," thickly, and Ashley, unable to help herself, put her fingers into Penny's hair.

"Look at you," she said hoarsely. "Perfect woman. Red lingerie. Keep it on, baby, please. And make me feel good, Penny. I'm so fucking hot for you right now I could just about scream."

"Please yes." Penny slid her hands up Ashley's hips, light delicate touch before she traced her thumb into Ashley's cleft, the bare skin there shrieking with sensitivity and anticipation. Penny's tongue, incredibly hot and soft, darted out, following where her thumb had traced, and Ashley gasped, fingers tightening in her mate's hair and her knees wobbling.

"Yes. Yes, good girl, God, yeah. Come on. Come on, I want it!"

Penny hummed but didn't delve any deeper, her tongue tracing over the delicate flesh, tasting slick wetness and teasing the creases as Ashley's voice lifted in whining demand. She still wasn't ready when Penny parted her cleft and drove her tongue deep. Her knees buckled, and Penny, anticipating it, caught some of Ashley's weight and helped her drop to the couch without falling. Then she pulled Ashley's hips forward, pushing her thighs wide, and explored her throbbing clit with the same attention to detail Ashley had used on her nipples.

Only it was better, or maybe worse, because that soft strong tongue and all that heat came so close, over and over again, to making her come, bringing her right up to the edge and then faltering as Ashley cried out and squirmed, knotting and loosening her hands in Penny's hair. "Come on come on fuck me make me come I need it, you're fucking teasing me oh god *god* Penny!"

Penny's soft laughter vibrated through her, and Ashley knew she was right, her mate *was* teasing her, and it was phenomenal. She babbled again, getting so close to release, pleading for it, and then, desperately, dropped her voice and said, "Fucking *now*, Penny, make me come now!"

That was what her mate was waiting for. The

command. All at once Penny's fingers were inside her, curving hard against the sweet spot on the pubic bone, and Ashley orgasmed so hard she saw stars. Her, "Yes, yes, again, *do* it, Penny!" was hoarse with pleasure, and it got what she demanded, staggering waves of pleasure slamming through her until she was quivering and exhausted with release. Clumsy, sated, thrilled, she dragged Penny back up onto the couch and wrapped her arms and legs around her, clinging and murmuring pleasured nonsense. Penny fumbled for a blanket from the back of the couch, and a little to Ashley's surprise, very quickly, they both slept.

"You," Penny rasped, quite a long nap later, "have got a *serious* 'lady in the streets, sex fiend in the sheets' thing going on here. I did *not* expect that."

Ashley, who was astonishingly comfortable to sleep on, made a small, almost embarrassed sound. "Too much?"

"Jesus, no, it was incredible, just not what I imagined." Penny squished around enough to steal a kiss, then, seeing Ashley's blush, kissed her jaw, too, and murmured, "I loved it. I've never really been with a dom woman before. I've only dated women who are into the whole 'short and bossy' thing. I didn't know *I* had it in me. It's good," she promised. "It's incredible."

Ashley shivered. "Okay. I don't usually come on that strong, I'm—" She shook her head. "I'm too big, too tall, too strong. I don't want to scare anybody. But I like to take charge."

"In everything," Penny said with a grin. "And you're good at it. And it seems to me like your fated mate is the perfect person to come on strong with. Fate must mean we're compatible, right? God," she added, distracted by her own thoughts. "Yeah, read me the phone book and then do *that* to me. I'm all in." She stole another kiss, then sighed contentedly. "I could stay here forever."

Ashley laughed quietly. "I thought we were going to come up with something better to read than a phone book. And yeah, I could too, except I think I might already be late for work."

"No. No way. Really? You?" Penny looked for a clock, then laughed and nuzzled at Ashley again. "I'm a bad influence. Letting your inner dom out and then making you late for work. But maybe you could use being a little less responsible? Just a little bit," she promised. "Let your hair down a bit and relax. Just a tiny bit."

Ashley, sounding offended, said, "I'm not uptight, am I?"

"No," Penny said, surprised. "Just dedicated to the task at hand." She shivered all over. "For the record, I'm a *huge* fan of being dedicated to this kind of task. But if you're late to work maybe we should shower. And I should try to get your clothes back from wherever missing shifter clothes go."

Ashley blinked, then laughed, and, sheepishly, said, "I forgot that's why we got naked in the first place."

Penny, firmly, said, "That is *not* why we got naked. It was just a really good excuse."

Ashley laughed again and pulled her up for a kiss, murmuring, "It was. And yes, shower. Together?"

"That will not get you to work anything like on time. Absolutely." Penny climbed off the couch and pulled Ashley up as well, and they managed to get through a shower without *too* much delay. Ashley dried her hair while Penny sat and concentrated on shifting to a partridge and then back again with the clothes she'd lost, but several tries netted her absolutely nothing.

"It's okay," Ashley said. "The dress was panic-levels of important. My skirt and shirt are not."

Penny wailed, "But!" and her partridge, startled, said, *Butts?*

Do partridges even know what butts are? Penny demanded.

The bird gazed at her with a distant, confused expression, then began scratching around in the landscape of Penny's mind like it was looking for bugs.

Maybe, Penny thought helplessly, it had thought she'd said 'bugs' to begin with. She dragged her brain away from bugs and said, "But your clothes," to Ashley, who came over to steal a kiss.

"It's honestly fine. I'm going to drive you back to your hotel so you can put your own clothes on, and then bring you to the pub so you can get your van, which is probably frozen solid, and after you've thawed it you can bring Karina's dress back to her and that'll be one thing less that you have to worry about."

"Do I have anything else to worry about? Besides finding your clothes?"

"Just Christmas Eve with five thousand Torbens," Ashley promised.

"Oh, that. It'll be fine." Penny grimaced, then widened her eyes. "But oh, wait. Are we telling them? Can I tell Gwen, at least? And she'll tell Bill, but will Bill tell anybody?"

"Not if Gwen tells him not to," Ashley said, sounding almost like she believed it. "But it's up to you, in general. If you want to tell them, we can. They'll be thrilled. But if you want to have some more time to come to terms with being a shifter yourself, that's also incredibly understandable and totally okay."

Penny held her breath a moment, then nodded. "Let's start with Gwen and Bill. See how that goes. I'll think about the other Torben hordes after that. T-horde-bens?"

Ashley laughed. "T-horde-bens, yeah. T-hordens. I like it."

EVEN ONE TORBEN, Penny decided a couple of hours later, was enough of a horde.

It wasn't Bill's fault he was about six and a half feet tall. Six eight with the pompadour. But it did make him a pretty credible horde, even all by himself. Particularly in winter gear, which everybody was wearing in Colorado at this time of year, bulking them all out. It was just that Bill didn't need any extra bulk to be very large, so he looked a bit like a bear walking on his hind feet when he came into the ice cream parlor where Penny was waiting for him and Gwen.

He is a bear on hind feet, her partridge pointed out, which was possibly the most sensible thing it had said so far. *But we can be bigger than him,* it added smugly. *I can be big. Want to see how bi—*

NO!!!

The partridge looked deeply offended and sank into the depths of Penny's mind with a sense of injured, sullen pride. Penny, trying to ignore it, waved Bill and Gwen down, and curled her hands around the mug of really excellent coffee she'd already picked up from the counter. Gwen bounced over to drop into the seat across from her. "I was going to say, you know it's nine degrees out, right? What are you doing inviting us to meet you at an ice cream shop?"

"I figured it wouldn't be busy. I was wrong!" It was a cozy little cafe with linoleum floors, walls painted with bright splashes of color, and booths that could fit anywhere from two to ten. There were a startling number of people there for the Saturday afternoon before Christmas. An even more startling percentage of them were actually eating ice cream, although they were also still all bundled against the cold, which made it even funnier. "But I wanted to talk to you away from the pub."

Gwen, who was pretty pale to begin with, paled rather dramatically. "Oh my God. You're not leaving the band, are you?"

Penny gaped at her. "No!"

"Oh, thank God." Gwen slumped so far in her seat that she nearly slid out of it. "Okay, God! Don't scare me like that!"

"I didn't! You came up with that entirely on your own! You scared yourself!"

The *damned* partridge fluttered up in Penny's mind in an absolute panic, wings and feathers going every-where. *RUN! RUN AWAY!* It put on a burst of speed, by partridge standards, and raced across whatever space it existed in within Penny, wings still flapping, although it didn't take off.

It took everything Penny had to stay still in her chair. *What is wrong with you?!?*

THERE'S SOMETHING SCARY!

Bewildered, Penny looked around the ice cream parlor. Bear-sized Bill, ordering ice cream and coffee at the counter, was the scariest thing in the cafe, and he was about as scary as a teddy bear. *There's nothing scary at all?*

THE LADY IS SCARED!

"She—" Penny strangled the sound. *Gwen* **scared** *herself by imagining things! Just like you're doing!*

No! I'm scared because she is! The partridge sent a

garbled idea of 'if the human is scared there must be a reason for a small bird to be scared,' followed by *I DON'T HAVE TO BE SMALL!*

Penny said, "No!" out loud this time, startling Gwen, who looked embarrassed.

"I heard you the first time. I don't know why I just decided you were quitting. That would be the worst."

"No, I—oh, God. I can't do this twice. Let's wait for Bill."

Gwen's eyes popped. "Oh my God. Are you *pregnant?*"

EGGS! WHERE ARE THE EGGS?!?! The partridge, apparently distracted from random fears, began scrabbling around in search of, Penny guessed, a nest. Eggs. Maybe chicks. She was so distracted by it that she could only say, "No," much less strenuously than before. Absently, even.

Gwen looks suspicious. "Are you sure? That should have gotten a way stronger reaction than 'are you quitting the band.'"

Chicks, the partridge said decisively, as if remembering. *Humans have chicks, not eggs. Where are the chicks?* Single-minded worry sent it scrambling around Penny's mind again, looking for chicks.

Penny groaned. *I don't have any chicks. Go to sleep.* Aloud, she said, "Yes. I mean, no. I mean, yes, I'm certain I'm not pregnant, and you're right, my reactions are all off, and—oh, thank God, Bill."

The big man lumbered over and sat, giving Penny

first a pleasant nod of greeting, then suddenly going still and staring at her like he'd never seen her before. Penny understood perfectly: she could *sense* that he was a shifter, somehow. It was almost as if she could see a glow around him, although she couldn't. Or feel an unusual warmth from him, maybe. That was closer, although still not exactly right. She just *knew*, basically, and it didn't make any sense.

"Penny?" Bill asked cautiously. "Are you, um, feeling all right?"

"Fine, yes, thank you."

We could be dying, the partridge said in sepulchral tones. *The bear probably senses it.* Its eyes widened. *It's going to eat us. We're easy prey. RUN AWAY!!!*

Penny whispered, "Oh my *God,*" and tried very, very hard to ignore the bird. "That's what I wanted to talk to you about," she said to Bill, and then, taking a deep breath, turned her gaze to Gwen and dropped her voice. "So I found out last night that I'm a shifter."

I can do that! the bird yelled in Penny's head. *Let's show her!*

"A—like Bill?" Gwen whispered, stunned.

Not like Bill! Like a bird! I can do that! Let's show her!

Oh look, Penny said inside her head, *Wonder Woman's jet is right over there. Go admire it.*

The partridge, to her huge relief, ran off in search of the jet. Maybe that would keep it busy for a while. "Not exactly like Bill," Penny admitted in a mumble. "I turn into a partridge."

"A p—" Gwen stopped on the popping sound of the *p* and swallowed. "Like your last name?"

"A horrible irony," Penny muttered. "I talked to some other shifters earlier today and they said I probably suppressed the ability for my own safety, because no one around me was one. Apparently it happens sometimes. Not often. They said it takes a huge amount of willpower."

Gwen's eyebrows rose. "Well, that describes you if it describes anybody I know."

The jet is gone! What's a jet? Where did it go?

A jet is a thing that flies through the air like a bird, Penny replied. *It's around here somewhere. Go look.*

The partridge ran off again, now with a vague bird-like image in its mind. Penny very carefully didn't think about how Wonder Woman's jet was, in fact, invisible and therefore impossible to find. Gwen put her hands out across the table, and Penny sank hers into them, grateful for the connection. "So I wanted to tell you. I wanted to tell you…"

Bill was squinting at her. "How did you figure it out, at this late stage? Did you shift for some reason?"

Penny gave him a nervous smile. "Well, see, Ashley showed me her bear—"

I CAN DO THAT!

Penny struggled not to let the wretched partridge shift in the middle of the cafe, blurting, "and my partridge thought 'I can do that,' and then it did, and everything's been kind of insane since."

*I **can** do that! Let me show them! You can do that! We can do it! Bees do it! Bears do it! Let's do it! We'll fall in love!*

Penny, helplessly, whispered, *Those aren't even the right lyrics,* and the partridge gazed at her in bewilderment.

What's a lyric?

Bill's face lit up. "There's only one reason I know that shifters usually tell true humans—or people we think are true humans—about our animals. Penny, is Ashley your mate?"

Gwen rolled her eyes so hard Penny was surprised they didn't plop out of her head and land on the table. "Your *true love,*" she muttered, although it was obviously meant affectionately. "I'm sorry, I just cannot take this 'mate' thing seriously. But does that mean she *is* your true love?"

Where? Where's our true love? Our mate should be watching the eggs. Sitting on them. Oh no, where are the chicks? The partridge gasped. *Maybe they're in the jet. The jet flies like a bird. Maybe it lays eggs. Partridge eggs!* It tore off looking for the jet again.

Penny clutched her head and nodded, trying both to be happy and to cope with the bird in her brain. "She is and it's wonderful and I'm thrilled but oh my *god,* guys, I don't think I suppressed my shifter abilities for safety. Or at least, not because I was afraid someone would find me out. I think I suppressed them because this bird is as *dumb as a box of rocks,* and if I let it loose in public it would walk out into traffic and get us both killed."

IS THE JET IN TRAFFIC? WITH THE CHICKS? WHAT'S TRAFFIC?

"Oh." Bill's eyes widened enormously. "Oh dear. That bad? I know non-predator shifter species can be..." He hesitated. "Flighty."

I can fly!!! The partridge ran like hell across the landscape of Penny's mine, launched itself into the air, and flapped along for several feet, just above the ground, before landing in a rolling thump. *Oooh, maybe the eggs are here!*

Penny gave a hollow laugh and described the bird's antics while Gwen sucked her cheeks in and tried hard not to laugh. "We've got to go somewhere that you can show me," she whispered. "Oh my God, Pen, this is amazing."

"Actually, that's a pretty good idea," Bill said. "Usually shifters get all this out of their systems before they can even remember, but since you came to it so late, you might just need to spend a while shifting back and forth a lot and letting the partridge run around."

"Are you telling me that because I've started shifting so late, I've got a bird too young to understand object permanence?"

Bill's eyes sparkled. "Yeah, maybe. I think you and Gwen should go out to—oh, I know. Uncle Jeff and Aunt Holly. They live up in the mountains. You can shift there without anybody seeing you. Ashley will bring you up."

"Ashley is insanely busy with work for the next seventy-two hours," Penny objected.

"I'll cover for her." Bill looked happy. "This is more important. And if you've got it under control by the family reunion, you can tell everybody there!"

"You want me to tell like nine hundred people at once?" Penny asked faintly. "That sounds terrifying."

"We're very nice," Bill promised. "Just large. Let me go cover for Ashley, and I promise, it's all going to be fine."

Ashley hadn't argued very much when Bill appeared at the pub and told her to bring Penny up into the mountains so her mate could practice shifting. She *had* said, "I'm not shirking my responsibilities," a little defensively, and her cousin had hauled her into what could only be described as a bear hug.

"You never would," he promised her. "I know that. But this is important, Ash. More important than the pub. Besides, you probably want your folks to meet her before the rest of the Torben crush, right? I said Gwen should go with you," he added, putting her back on her feet. "Mostly because they've known each other a long time and Penny could probably use the stability of having an old friend around. If you think that's a bad idea—"

"No, it sounds smart," Ashley admitted. "How'd Gwen take it?"

"She's thrilled," Bill said happily. "Congrats, Ash. I'm

really happy for you. Now get going. Gwen and Penny are waiting for you out in the car."

Ashley had gotten going, and a little to her amazement, had been entertained on the 45 minute drive out to her folks' house by an a cappella, two-woman *Sixty Pix* concert, broken up by Gwen's giggles over her own terrible puns, and occasionally by Penny's wail of despair at her partridge.

It'll be fine, right? she asked her bear as she drove the last mile or so through the snowy woods out to the secluded house. *Poor Penny will get used to it? Or Bill's right and her partridge will mature?*

The bear, usually so reassuring and calm, gave a great languid shrug. *Penny will be all right, but...prey animals.* It gave another shrug, as if saying, 'what can you do?'

A moment later they were pulling up to her parents' house, so Ashley let it go as first her mom, then her dad, came out of the log cabin nestled up against the mountainside. Ashley couldn't help smiling as she waved a greeting, loving the way warm light glowed out the windows, making the house look like a welcoming beacon in the dark. "Ash?" her mom yelled. "Everything okay, baby?"

"It's fine, Mom, I've just got somebody for you to meet!"

Her mother said, "Oh my God, Jeff," to her dad. "She's finally met somebody."

"I'm twenty-eight," Ashley yelled. "That is not old to

meet somebody!" More quietly, to Penny, she said, "I'm sorry in advance."

Penny, bundling out of the car, laughed. "It'll be fine, as long as they—*no,* they are *not* going to hunt you even if they *are* bears! They're bears, right?"

"They are. Both of them. I'm surprised they're awake, honestly. They keep threatening to go down for a nap in mid-December and not get up again until March. Mom says it's a great diet plan. Not only sleep through the holiday food extravaganza, but also burn off all the body fat she padded on during the rest of the year."

"That would be so amazingly unhealthy if they were human," Penny muttered. Ashley laughed an agreement, then walked her and Gwen up to the door to meet her parents.

"Mom, Dad, this is Penny and Gwen. Penny—" She hesitated, suddenly shy about revealing the truth, since Penny had been through so much in the past day.

Penny, though, offered a hand to her mom and said, "It turns out I'm Ashley's mate, which would be enough of a surprise, but yesterday I didn't even know I was a shifter, so we were hoping I could just sort of practice in your yard for a while."

Ashley's mom shrieked gleefully and threw her arms around Penny with such enthusiasm that it nearly knocked the drummer over. Ashley's bear gave a warning grumble, but Penny wasn't really in danger, just staggering a bit. "I'm Holly," Ashley's mom all but yelled in Penny's ear. "I'm so happy to meet you! This is

Jeff! How could you not know you were a shifter? Come in, come in, tell us everything and have some dinner and then yes, of course, practice all you want. I'm Holly," she repeated to Gwen. "And you're Bill's mate, aren't you? He said you were striking."

Ashley's dad herded them inside with an apologetic glance at Gwen, who was beaming cheerfully. "Don't mind me," she told him. "I'm loving all of this. And I love your house."

"Thank you. Holly and I built it."

"No way!" Gwen's jaw dropped and she slowed down, exclaiming over the log wall exterior and the huge, triple-paned windows that let so much light glow onto the snow outside. The inside was just as cozy, with plastered walls and open-beamed ceilings, and wood floors littered with rugs. Ashley mostly didn't notice any of that anymore, but as kids, she and her brothers had loved hitting those rugs at a run, shifting as they did so, and skidding down the hallways while their mother yelled at them.

Her mom had tucked her arm through Penny's and was getting all the details, complete with dismayed cooing sounds as Penny explained her partridge's half-wittedness. Ashley drifted along in their wake, listening to Penny and her mom, and to Gwen and her dad, feeling an unbelievable sense of contentedness rising up inside herself. She had so many ambitions, but she thought of them as being centered around the pub, around making the business she'd taken over a success. It hadn't occurred to her that she had as-powerful ambitions to build a satisfactory *life* for herself, one with friends and lovers and family, but right now, in the midst of all that, she could recognize the ambition as beginning to be satisfied.

She might not even be annoyed at the last-minute family reunion, looking at it that way. The idea made her chuckle as her parents led them into the big, bright kitchen that was the heart of their home.

Ashley loved that space. The cabinetry was hand-built and wooden, with glass-fronted doors that made it easy to see what was where. It had extra-deep counters, giving her dad, who liked to bake, two feet of workspace *plus* the space needed to store canisters and crockery against the red-tile backsplash. Most of the appliances were red, making striking accents to the cream-colored counters and golden wood cabinets. There was a big island with a secondary sink in it, bar stools around it, and, at the moment, a gloriously fluffy-looking lemon meringue pie sitting smack in the middle of it.

Ashley laughed, seeing it. "You were about to each eat an entire half of a lemon meringue pie, weren't you?"

Her mother didn't even look guilty. "They're best the day they were made. You're lucky you didn't get here ten minutes later."

Penny, awed, said, "You *made* a lemon meringue pie? I don't even think I knew that could be done. I thought they only got made in restaurants, or something."

"Jeff made it," Ashley's mom said rather smugly.

"You're in for a treat, if you've never had homemade before. How handy that the recipe suggests cutting it into five pieces."

"Instead of two," Ashley said, still laughing. Her mother stuck her tongue out and cut generous pieces of pie for everyone.

Penny oohed and aahed her way through hers, finally turning to Ashley. "Do you know how to make these?"

"Yes? It's not hard, just a little time consuming."

"I have the best mate in the world," Penny announced to Ashley's delight and the objection of everyone else in the room.

"Go practice your shifting," her dad said after a while. "I'll clean up in here and get the guest room ready. For Gwen," he clarified. "Ashley and Penny can sleep in Ash's room."

"Please don't judge me for my high school obsessions," Ashley muttered, but they went out to the back yard so Penny could practice her shifting. Fortunately, she remembered her clothes every time, probably because it was a few degrees below zero up there on the mountainside.

"It doesn't help," she eventually groaned. "The partridge is still distracted by everything, can't remember what happened two seconds ago, and flips out if it hears something it didn't expect, even if it was something I was just thinking or talking about! Can shifter animals just be...*dumb*?"

"True animals can be," Ashley said, thinking of a

spectacularly dumb, if sweet, cat they'd had when she was growing up. "I guess I don't know why shifter animals couldn't be, except usually they have enough of their human part in them to keep from being really stupid, I think."

Penny fell backward into a snow drift, making angel wings and then letting out a frustrated squawk as she shifted to partridge form and beat at the snow like it had offended her. She turned back to human, spluttered, "It thought the snow was attacking me!" and threw her hands in the air. "*I'm* not dumb, am I? Pretty drummer hit things hard, go 'urgh?'" She did a very credible caveman grunt at the end of that.

Gwen, watching from up on the cabin's back deck, laughed. "No. No, you're not dumb. Nobody who can handle social media the way you do is dumb. Or who comes through with flying organizational skills in an emergency. Or—"

Penny sat up abruptly. "Does my partridge have ADHD?! No," she said before either Ashley or Gwen could answer. She collapsed back into the snow, looking disappointed. "No, it doesn't feel like that. Not what it feels like in my brain, anyway. It's not that it...well, maybe it *is* reacting before it thinks. Emotion before intellect. But it doesn't get distracted from its fixation...oh, maybe that too," she admitted. "The whole egg thing. It kept coming back to the eggs. Oh my God. Maybe my partridge *does* have ADHD." She lay there a minute, clearly thinking that over as she puffed steamy breath into the air, and finally added, "But it's also dumb. It thinks the air is on fire."

Ashley couldn't help giggling at that last. She went over to drop into the snow next to Penny and held her hand. "So how do you deal with ADHD?"

"How do *I* deal with it? Meds. How does a partridge deal with it? I have no idea." Penny sighed another steamy breath toward the sky. "I'm pretty sure 'dumb' is the bigger part of the problem here. 'Fire! Fire! Run away from the fire! It's too cold for fire! What's burning? Find a nest! Is the nest burning? What about the eggs?!'"

She was clearly quoting the partridge, its scatter-brained alarm fluctuating through the words. Ashley's bear rumbled, *Calm,* and put its paw over Penny's chest.

Actually put its paw over her chest, as Ashley shifted into bear form without intending to, and sat beside Penny in the snowbank, one massive paw pressed gently against Penny's torso. She inhaled a sharp squeak, then, audibly surprised in a different way, breathed, "Oh," and relaxed like she'd just gone into a sauna.

Calm, Ashley repeated. *Now shift.* She lifted her paw so Penny could shift without being crushed, although Penny obviously remembered what Ashley didn't, in the moment: that she could shift into a truly enormous partridge. Gwen, up above them, said, "Holy shit!" as Penny transformed into a bird roughly the same size as Ashley's grizzly, although nothing like in her weight class. Still, a bird some eight feet from nose to tail feathers was shockingly large, and when Penny spread her wings to adjust her balance, even Ashley, as a bear, took an awed breath. Penny's wingspan had to be a solid twenty feet across, and even if birds had light-weight bones, Ashley would *not* want to be smacked by one of those wings.

Or raked by one of those *feet*. They were long and spindly and had appalling-looking claws at the ends, visible as Penny lifted her feet and put them back down again, settling herself, then cocked her head to stare at Ashley.

Ashley, or her bear, murmured, *Good,* then leaned forward to gently bump her huge furry head against Penny's feathery one. The bird's neck retracted into a fluff of feathers at the weight of Ashley's head, and she tried to adjust to use less pressure. After a moment, Penny extended her neck again a little, looking more comfortable. Ashley said, *Good,* again. *It's all right. You're safe. You're whole now. I know you've been hidden for a long time, but everything is okay now.*

There was a silence, one that Ashley didn't know what to do with. Her bear, serene and mellow as always, was content to wait, and after a little while, to her complete astonishment, she heard Penny—or Penny's partridge—whisper, *Ashley?*

Yes, the bear said. *Your mate.*

Penny, as amazed as Ashley, said, *I didn't know we could talk like this.*

Ashley gave a big rumbling bear chuckle. The Ashley part of her said, *Neither did I!* and the bear, calm and confident, said, *We don't, often. The human parts of us are so good at talking, it's easier to let them do it for us. But you've been hidden so long,* it said gently. *You need some time to breathe. Time to know who you are. Time to know you're not alone. So you need to hear me. Your mate,* it said again, fondly.

The partridge didn't answer. Not in words, at least. She did press her head against Ashley's, clearly using a lot of partridge weight and strength, but the truth was, even an eight-foot-long bird couldn't budge a bear. Ashley's mind wandered a moment, wondering how much ostriches weighed, and whether *they* could press hard enough to move her, but she let the thought go. Partridges weren't built like ostriches, anyway.

After a long time, the partridge sighed and very quietly said, *It's not safe.*

It wasn't, Ashley's bear agreed. *It is now. You're safe. I'll keep you safe.*

She could feel that Penny trusted her. That the partridge trusted her. But she could also feel all the time the shifter part of her had been hidden and quiet, not trusting the world. It would take a long time, she thought, before the partridge really felt *safe.*

That's all right, the bear said, still gently. *We have all the time we need. Your human is a good fierce protector. **She** kept you safe, even without knowing it. Now she has me, and you are,* the bear said again, ***safe***. *No one will ever hurt my mate.*

All at once, unexpectedly, Penny shifted back to human, her eyes soft and huge and grateful. She put both hands on Ashley's face, very small and soft in all the rough bear fur, and when Ashley shifted, too, Penny smiled and stole a kiss, whispering, "I'm awfully tired. I think it's time to go in now."

Ashley slipped her arm around Penny's shoulders and guided her back to the house, murmuring, "Of course. Anything for you, Penny. Anything for you."

CHAPTER 22

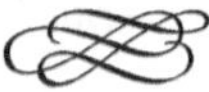

*P*enny didn't actually shift for the entirety of the next two days, but a lot of the time, it felt like it. She did sleep a lot, and in between, she ate a lot. Ashley's mom, Holly, was a good cook, and her husband Jeff was an incredible baker. And when she wasn't sleeping or eating, she was practicing shifting.

The clothes she'd borrowed from Ashley were literally a lost cause, but she didn't lose any more. The partridge settled down some as she got used to shifting. Whenever being totally overwhelmed by it all started to creep up on her, Penny remembered Ashley's huge soft furry head pressing gently against hers, the bear's rich gentle voice calming her. It was like a blanket of reassurance she could draw around herself, making everything less panicky, even when Ashley had to go to work in the evenings. Penny didn't mind staying with her parents for a couple of days: everyone had been right about how much easier it became with some time to practice.

The partridge, unfortunately, remained dumb. Less panicky, but dumb. Penny read a lot about birds over the days she stayed with Ashley's parents. It turned out that 'bird-brained' wasn't really an insult at all: bird brains were unbelievably complex, their ability to navigate in the air as well as on the ground requiring a genuinely amazing cognitive power.

Partridges, however, were not known for their flight abilities. They were ground birds, and although her kind—red-legged partridges—could get into trees, they mostly didn't. They probably weren't dumber than any other average bird, either, but the truth was, Penny's partridge was not a shining example of its type. "Shouldn't that mean *I'm* dumb too?" she half-wailed at Ashley on the morning of Christmas Eve.

"Obviously not," Ashley said, amused. "We'll have to find you some other non-predator-shifters to talk to. Maybe it's not so much dumb as just…cautious."

Penny sighed. "It spent twenty minutes last night obsessed over the straw in your parents' Nativity scene."

Straw! the partridge said, suddenly alert. *Good for nests!*

For what felt like the hundredth time, Penny said, *It's ceramic. Not good for nests.*

The partridge cocked its head at her, one eye and then the other, exactly as it had done the night before, and in its mind, pecked at the straw before wailing, *The straw hurts my face!* as if this was a brand-new revelation.

Ashley tried very hard not to laugh as Penny mournfully repeated the investigation and conversation aloud. "The only reason it stopped last night was it thought the Christmas tree lights might be a fire, or the sun, or possibly—"

A snack!!! The partridge provided an image of green and yellow bugs, about the same size as an LED tree light, and apparently its idea of the world's most delicious snack. *Not mine,* it said severely. *Good for chicks.*

Penny sighed. "A snack. It thinks they look like something chicks would snack on. You know, it might be dumb, but it's really focused on nests and safety and food. It might be a good parent. Although I don't know how that would work, with me expecting to be on the road a lot."

Ashley rolled onto her back, dragging Penny with her. "You know...I'm not going on the road with you, right?"

Penny pushed up on an elbow, frowning down at Ashley. "Yeah, I mean, you've got a full-on job here...?"

Ashley sighed, relaxing. "Yeah. I do. And it's not that I mind the idea of traveling some, but I'm a homebody. I like to have my roots down. I know Bill's given up a lot for Gwen..."

"Has he, though?" Penny flopped down. "The way I understand it he was going nuts trying to run two businesses and even if Gwen hadn't come along he would have needed somebody to take over the pub. So that's not really giving it up for her. And Gwen says the brewery itself doesn't need as much day-to-day supervision, and that coming along with the band sometimes means he can use that as a chance to sell Thunder Bear beer to other places. So is it really giving all that much up? It's just a change. And, look." She kissed Ashley's jaw. "I don't want to ask you to give anything up either. The band is going to have to figure out where we want to be based if Gwen and I both end up moving to Renaissance—"

Ashley squeaked and Penny pushed up on her elbow again, laughing. "Well, wouldn't that make the most sense? Your life is here and I bet even people in Renaissance need housecleaners."

"Or crime scene cleaners," Ashley mumbled.

Penny laughed again. "Again with the preferring not to have trauma. No, really, Ash. I may have to go into Denver for three nights a week so we can practice, but yeah, I'm thinking my home base should be here. Where you are." She gave the blonde woman a dippy smile. "With my mate."

Ashley squeaked again and pulled Penny down into a hard hug. "You should think about it, not make any rash decisions—"

"Right," Penny mumbled into her cleavage, "because there's nothing rash about magically assured love at first sight or suddenly changing into partridges."

"—but I've been—" Ashley caught up to what Penny had said and fought down giggles. "Well, yeah. The shifter world isn't quite like the true human world, is it? Anyway, I've been worried since the first time I saw you, Pen. How was that going to work? I thought maybe I was wrong about the mate bond, because… how could it work?"

"It'll work just fine," Penny promised. "We'll figure it out."

"In that case there's only one more huge hurdle to leap," Ashley said into her hair. "The Ten Thousand Torbens Christmas Eve."

THERE WERE NOT *REALLY* ten thousand Torbens. Penny knew it. If they would all hold still for a minute, in fact, she was almost positive there were a very countable number of them.

One, the partridge said desperately. *Seventeen. Ninety-two. Four.*

Four, Penny agreed. *Nineteen. Seventy-two.*

Oddly enough, that settled the partridge down a little. So did Penny whispering, "That one's Jon," to herself. "That one's Bill, he's easy, he's got the pompadour. Well, and also Gwen's hanging on his arm, and I've known him for months now. That's Luke, he's the really blonde one. That's Laurie," she said with a dubious glance at the other long-haired Torben man who was right about Ashley's age. "Maybe I've got Jon and Laurie mixed up."

"They're the idiots," Ashley said fondly as she came

over with a couple of beers and heard the last of that. "Jon's hair is darker and Laurie's mouth is fuller."

"If you say so," Penny muttered just before she sipped the beer. "Dang, that's really good. Is that the Thunder Blunder?"

"Laurie's speciality." Ashley nodded. "He was trying to hurry something along and reinvented a crystal malt. What are they *doing*?" The answer to that was obviously 'getting hot wings ready to eat,' but she ignored her own question, going on with, "How many others can you identify?"

Penny snorted. "Your mom and dad. Bill's mom and dad. Cassidy over there, but only because there aren't nearly as many girls as there are boys. I know most of the rugged older men must be your dad's brothers, but besides Bill's dad, I don't know which is which. There are like *seventy* of you, Ashley! And you all look alike!"

The partridge popped an image of a bunch of partridges in a row into Penny's mind. The birds all looked more less identical. *We look alike too! We're cute!*

Despite herself, Penny laughed. *Bears are pretty cute, too.*

*Bears are **dangerous**,* the bird informed her.

If not friend, why friend-shaped?

That was too much for the partridge. It stared at her, then tucked his head under its wing and ignored her.

"It'll be fine," Ashley promised. "Nobody expects you to remember everybody tonight."

"But they all know who I am!"

Ashley gazed down at her with sympathetic amusement. "You do stand out, Pen."

"Because I'm five two and you're all eleven feet tall! I
don't stand out, I'm a small herbivore who can be easily
squished by the rampaging ungulates!"

There was a long pause as Ashley visibly tried not
to laugh, and clearly struggled not to correct everything Penny had just said. *We'll be squished*, the
partridge said sadly.

"Bears aren't ungulates," Ashley finally managed.

"And they don't rampage and partridges aren't
herbivores." Penny stuck her lip out. "You know what I
mean, though."

Ashley bent to kiss that pouty lip and bumped her
nose against Penny's. "I do. I also want you to
remember you can shift into a partridge fourteen feet
high at the shoulder and gut any bear in this room."

Penny brightened. "You think?"

"Yes. You can start with my idiot cousins," Ashley
said as Jon and Laurie put effort into waving them
down. "Do you want to see what they want, or should
we pretend we didn't see them?"

"Since they're two of the ten people in this room I
can identify, let's see what they want." Beer in hand,
Penny dragged Ashley through the crowd to a table,
where her cousins had laid out a generous spread of
hot wings. Ashley took a deep breath and her eyes
started watering as Penny leaned over the table and
examined the wings appreciatively. "I love hot wings.
You guys make these?"

"Yep." Jon slid into the booth and gestured for Ashley and Penny to sit in the other side. "This is it. We're gonna settle the question of who screamed too much once and for all."

Penny, already sliding into the booth, laughed. "The question of what?"

Ashley froze and stepped back. "I told you I'm *done* with that argument."

Laurie tied his hair back with a dramatic action and sat next to his brother. "So when we were kids," he said to Penny, "we went to Disneyland."

Penny brightened. "Oh my God. Is this the Disneyland Incident Ashley mentioned? I must hear this!"

Ashley, with a groan, said, "*No.* Dudes, we settled this at Disneyland, it wasn't a big deal."

"It was totally a big deal," Jon said. "So we went on one of the roller coasters," he said to Penny. "And we're all, like, nine, right? So prime screaming ages."

"Only *Ashley*," Laurie said in critical tones, "screamed and screamed and *screamed*. So much that me and Jon didn't get a chance to."

Penny burst out laughing, saw they were serious, and laughed again, even more loudly. "You don't have to take turns screaming on a roller coaster!"

"That's what I said!" Ashley half-shouted. "We had to go on it again so they could scream!"

"But she didn't let us." Jon narrowed his eyes dramatically at his cousin, who still hadn't sat down.

"Of course I didn't!" Ashley said indignantly. "You don't have to take turns screaming on a roller coaster!"

"So you see what we've had to put up with all these years," Laurie said to Penny. "She won't take responsibility for her actions. But we're gonna settle this once and for all. The team who eats their way through the hottest wings without giving up wins the debate *and*," he said with a bright hopefulness in his eyes, "has to bring the other team to Disneyland so they can scream all they want."

Ashley said, "Absolutely not" at the same time Penny said, "Oh, you're *on*."

"Penny!"

"We're getting a free trip to Disneyland out of this!" Penny protested. "C'mon, sit down, we can take these guys!"

"I'm a total hot wings weenie and they know it! That's why they're challenging us to this dumb thing! No way! I already know I'm right! I don't need to settle up some twenty-year 'beef' here because it's obvious everybody can scream at the same time on a roller coaster!"

Laurie sniffed. "Chicken."

"Yeah, chicken *wings*," Penny shot back. "Roll out the milk bottles, babies, you're gonna need it."

"Penny!"

Penny beamed up at her girlfriend. "Trust me, Ash. We've got this." Her partridge was eyeing the table with cautious interest and spreading its wings. *Hot wings?*

Different from yours, Penny assured it.

Yes, the partridge agreed. *My wings are not hot. They are feathery.*

That's right, pal. Penny laughed as Ashley, with a groan, sat down.

Her cousins threw their hands in the air, cheering. "Hot! Wings! Hot! Wings! Hot! Wings! YEAAAAH!"

They drew attention despite the general noise in the pub. Gwen came over to the table, Bill trailing along behind her, and raised her eyebrows. "You guys are having a hot-wings-eating competition?" She laid a twenty on the table. "I got twenty on the girls."

Laurie stood up, shouting, "We got ourselves a *bet* going on here! C'mon, come lay your money down, girls versus boys, who can handle the hot? Watch us settle a twenty-year-old beef with the most ruthless competition of all! Ladies and gentlemen, come on down!"

Penny, laughing, leaned against Ashley's shoulder. "Is this what he's like at the faires?"

Ashley, glumly, said, "Yeah. He's great at pulling in a crowd. Pen, honestly, I'm *terrible* with hot foods."

"Only like ten people have ever tapped out of that hot wings celebrity thing," Penny said cheerfully, "and I think only one of them was a woman. The odds are totally in our favor."

"I'm going to die." Ashley put her head on the table and Penny, laughing, rubbed her back.

"It'll be fine. I promise. Would your mate lie to you?"

CHAPTER 23

*N*o, Ashley's bear said miserably as she bit into the third of seven escalatingly-hot wings. *Our mate would not **lie** to us, but she might be **wrong**...*

Ashley couldn't even answer the animal who lived in her own head. The first wings hadn't been too bad. The second were pretty spicy. The third had snot running down her nose and tears spilling from her eyes. She croaked, "I'm going to die," again, and reached for the glass of milk past a considerable pile of money on the table. Almost the entire family had gone in on the betting, and were now crowded around the booth, standing on chairs, tables, and other booths so they could watch. At least five people were filming them. Ashley's mouth felt like someone had stuck burning embers in it, and there were four more wings to go.

The only consolation was that Jon and Laurie were nearly as red-faced and weepy as she was. Laurie hadn't yet gone for the milk, but he was eyeing it, and Jon was bracing himself for the fourth wing.

Penny, casually, insolently, reached across the table and took the remains of Laurie's third wing, and ate it while maintaining eye contact with him. Then she licked her fingers and quirked an eyebrow at Jon, as if asking him if he really had the stones to eat another wing.

She hadn't been kidding about loving hot wings, or spice in general. She hadn't even broken a sweat, much less started crying. Jon actually faltered as she wiped her hands and nodded at his wings, challenging him to keep going. He set his jaw, and Laurie, in a fit of bravado, grabbed a wing and ate it in two fast bites. He didn't say anything, but even through the blur of spice-induced tears, Ashley could see him setting his face in a 'so there!' expression. Jon, more cautious, took a bite of his fourth wing and relaxed a little. "This one's not so bad."

Ashley said, "Oh, thank god," hoarsely, and bit into hers. He was right: it had a smokey heat to it, a delicious edge that made her take a second bite more eagerly.

Across the table, Laurie's face suddenly flushed bright red and tears erupted from his eyes as he started to cough. "Oh my God. Oh my God, it comes on after a minute there, oh my God."

It was too late to get rid of the bites she'd taken. The edge of smokiness in the wing suddenly deepened into a coal fire as it slid down her throat and hit her belly like a boiler being stoked. Jon was wheezing and hot-faced too, sweat beading at his temples as the heat hit him, too. Ashley dropped what was left of her wing, grabbing for the milk again. Penny, lazily, picked up the wing meant for her and took a savagely large bite of it, her eyes widening. "Oh, wow, that's *good*. Is there more?" She actually stood halfway up, as far as she could in the booth, and looked around the collected Torbens like somebody might be hiding hot wings from her.

"Just wait," Jon rasped. "Wait until it hits you. Oh, god, Laurie, this was a dumb idea."

"I *told* you," Ashley snapped. Her bear was lying on its back, mouth open, paws trying to scrape the heat off its tongue. "It's a stupid idea over a dumb beef that isn't even real!"

"I will *pay* for your whole Disneyland trip if you eat another plate of those," one of her relatives said admiringly. Penny, disappointed, finished her wing, stole the rest of Ashley's, and reached for the fifth one without even taking a drink of water.

Ashley, Jon and Laurie all watched in disbelief as she chowed down on that and went on to the final two with undiminished enthusiasm, only pausing before the last to say, "Aren't you guys gonna have yours?"

"How is your head not exploding?" Laurie whispered. He took his fifth wing, eyes tearing up as he inhaled its scent, and cast Jon a miserable look before biting into it. His pained, "Oh my God," was muffled by the wing. "We shouldn't have gotten the one called 'Gut Buster,' Jon."

Ashley wailed, "I'm eating something called 'Gut Buster?'" as she tried the fifth wing. Her bear had its head in a spring now, and was bellowing pain and outrage into the cold water. Ashley only wished it helped.

"C'mon, Ash," Penny said encouragingly. "It's just two more. And I'll eat your leftovers."

"I'm going to *die*! How are you doing this?"

"I told you, I like spice!" Penny actually managed to leer as she said it, which would have been really impressive if Ashley could respond instead of squirting tears and gasping sobs between each bite. "The sixth one is called 'Hellfire's Kitchen' and it's got a flavor like those red-hot candies we used to eat as kids? Or at least I did."

"That doesn't sound so bad." Jon took his sixth wing, bit into it, and just started to cry. Laurie stared at him, then at Penny, and then at Ashley as she, with trembling hands, took her own Hellfire's Kitchen wing and managed a tentative nibble. Her face flushed so hot she felt the tears spring to her eyes, just as was happening to Jon, and a cheer erupted around the table as Laurie shook his head and pushed his wings away. Penny delighted, grabbed both of his last two wings and ate them happily while Jon stared dismally at the seventh wing in front of him.

"Be real," he said to Penny. "How bad is it?"

Ashley, in a fit of stupidity, grabbed hers and took a

big enough bite to prove she'd done it, then let out a high thin squeak of horror and grabbed for her milk, too. And knocked it over, howling in dismay as it spilled. "No oh god no I'll die!"

"You can have mine," Penny said generously, and slid it to her.

Ashley drained the entire glass while her relatives, laughing and cheering, scrambled to clean up the mess she'd made. When she could breathe again, which took about four hours by Ashley's estimation, she wheezed, "Do you remember getting poison ivy when we were seven?" At Jon's cautious nod, she said, "Like that, except burning its way down your throat into your gut," and Jon, with a shudder, pushed his last wing away.

Penny pounced on it with a trill of delight while the gathered Torbens burst into a new round of cheers, jeers, and good-natured paying-up of debts. "Ladies and gentlemen," Ashley said through the fire in her throat, "let me introduce you to my mate, Penny Partridge, Champion Hot Wings Eater."

Another cheer went up, this one more sentimental-sounding as her family—those who hadn't already known—realized what she'd said and started swooping in for hugs and congratulations. "Is it in the water?" somebody asked. "Do I need to be introduced to the rest of the Sixty Pix?"

Penny heard that, and laughed. "The rest of us are either dating each other or not on the dating scene at all. I'm afraid you'll have to look elsewhere."

"Aw, well, congratulations anyway!"

Laurie's eyes were still watering as he tried, somewhat feebly, to get out of the booth. "The Gut Buster got me. I'm going to barf."

The crowd cleared out immediately, letting him through, and Ashley put her hand into Penny's, pulling her out of the booth. She said, "Aww, no more wings?" with apparent sincerity, although Ashley's stomach was roiling and she couldn't imagine wanting to eat more wings. Or anything else again. Ever.

We have to eat again, her bear said miserably. *We need to be nice and fat to hibernate.*

I can't hibernate, Ashley replied, almost as miserably. *My belly is too rotten.*

The poor bear moaned agreement and Ashley vowed to never, ever eat hot wings again for any reason at all. One of the cousins offered her another glass of milk and she drank it carefully, still hanging on to Penny's hand before whispering, "Thanks," hoarsely. "Oh my God, that was just awful."

"It was amazing," her cousin Luke disagreed. "Jon had been crowing about this idea for two days and he was sure you guys wouldn't make it past two wings."

"It's not true," Jon said from the booth, where he'd put his head on the table. "I thought you'd make it to four but I thought the Gut Buster would kill you, not me. I'm going to die."

"Don't underestimate girl power," Penny said smugly. "But also, don't die, that would ruin our whole Christmas Eve."

Jon lifted his head, looking injured. "Just your Christmas Eve?"

"Well, sure, you can't expect us to be all sad for you *tomorrow*, too, can you? Drink some milk," Penny suggested. "I think it's helping Ashley."

"She's just ruthless," another cousin said to Ashley, admiringly. "I'm not pressuring you, swear to God, but if you guys decide to have kids she's not gonna be the sympathetic mom, is she?"

Penny grinned. "Not if they challenge me to a hot-wings-eating contest, anyway!" She offered her hand, and the cousin—Jeremy—introduced himself, then turned to the next cousin and introduced him, too.

Ashley burped horribly, eyes watering, and whispered, "Oh, God, I think I need to run to the bathroom. I'm sorry, Pen, I don't mean to abandon you to this crew."

"I'll manage," Penny promised. "Go, feel better."

Ashley nodded, then bolted for the bathrooms.

CHAPTER 24

*P*enny worked her way through the crowd once Ashley left, greeting people, accepting congratulations, and forgetting names as soon as she was introduced. Everybody wanted to meet her, and nobody seemed to mind she couldn't remember who most of them were. They were even decent enough to let her go stand at the bar once she'd gotten through them all, and to give her a few minutes to recombobulate.

They were nice, thank goodness. There were just so many of them.

"It's totally overwhelming, isn't it?" A woman who wasn't a shifter came to stand next to Penny companionably. She was in her late fifties, curvy, and dressed rather gorgeously in Christmasy colors that flattered her skin tones. "I'm Pam. My husband is Richard, the big one over there with the good hair."

"That describes every man in the room," Penny said dryly.

Pam laughed. "I know, but let's be real, you wouldn't remember which one he was anyway, would you?"

"I probably will eventually!"

"Yeah. Eventually." Pam smiled at her. "For now, just let it all rush over you like—"

GIANT STOMPING ELEPHANT FEET!

"How do you even know what an elephant is?" Penny asked under her breath.

The partridge looked offended. ***You*** *know what an elephant is.*

I know what a Christmas tree light and a ceramic haystack in a manger are too, but that doesn't seem to have made any impression on you!

The partridge drew itself up into as regal a stance as a small brown bird with red markings could manage. *Elephants,* it said with dignity, *can stomp you.*

That was difficult to argue with, although Penny had the urge to try. Pam distracted her, though, with a tentative, "They're saying you just recently discovered you were a shifter?"

Penny squinched her face but couldn't help a laugh. "And here Ashley had been trying to convince me they *weren't* all talking about me. Yes, just a few days ago. Ashley's been helping me through it."

"What's it like?" Pam asked with a mix of curiosity and longing.

That sent a piercing thread of compassion through Penny. "It's a lot, isn't it?" she asked softly. "Not being a shifter in a room like this? How long ago did you meet Richard?"

"A little over thirty years. My whole life has been surrounded by shifters ever since. I gather it's not quite as crazy for people whose mates don't have enormous families, but it does make you feel a little left out sometimes. What does it feel like?"

"Weird. Annoying. Kind of cool. I think it would just feel ordinary, though, if I'd grown up this way. It feels—" Penny hesitated, considering it. "It does feel like a question has been answered, kind of. Like I was missing something that I didn't know *was* missing. But for what it's worth, if I'd never found out about it, I'm not sure I would have felt like I was missing anything. It's just this sort of additional weird thing about me, not the answer to everything about who I am. I was already that person. I just have a worried partridge in my head now."

Pam laughed, then tipped her head thoughtfully. "Thank you. It *is* ordinary for all of them, so I could never ask, but the rest of us who aren't shifters have always wondered amongst ourselves. Whether..."

"Whether you were less than they were?" Penny asked quietly. "You're not. A little different, that's all. I've spent my whole life hiding so well that not even I knew I was a shifter, and now that I know, I still have to hide. I don't think either is better, true human or shifter. There are just different constraints that come along with both of them."

"That's what Rich always says, but it's different,

hearing it from someone who spent their whole life being human up until now." Pam leaned her shoulder into Penny's in a friendly way. "Thank you. So," she added more brightly, "how's fated-matedness treating you?"

"Pretty great," Penny admitted dippily. "Ashley's… she's everything."

Pam beamed at her. "Good. Hold on to that, and enjoy your happily ever after. That's the best thing about it all. Knowing, without a doubt, that they're the right choice for you. The best one in the whole world, for you. And speaking of fate…"

A tall, handsome Torben man came up to bow theatrically and offer his hand. "Would you care to dance, Mrs Torben?"

"I would be delighted, Mr Torben." Pam put her hand into the man's, smiled at Penny, and went off to join a floor full of joyfully, if not elegantly, dancing shifters.

Ashley reappeared as Pam left, and slid her hands around Penny's waist. "You want to dance?"

"Horizontal mambo, maybe," Penny said, to Ashley's snerk of surprise.

"Not in front of eighty of my relatives, Pen."

"You've got the keys to the staff room, don't you?"

"So do at least nine other people here!"

Penny gave her mate a wicked smirk. "Adds to the spice."

"I have had *enough* spice for tonight."

Penny laughed. "Coward."

"Yes, but only because I've been a shifter long enough to know that shifters have excellent senses of smell *and* hearing and I can one hundred percent guarantee you there would not be a single soul at this party who didn't know exactly what we'd been up to, and what we'd said to each other while we were doing it."

"Oh, dear God. Okay, right, the regular ol' dance floor it is."

"Wait, though." Ashley pulled her closer and gazed down at her in bewilderment. "How did you even do that? My guts are still burning. I think they're going to keep burning for the rest of the month."

"Luckily it's the 24th," Penny said cheerfully. "Only a week of burning left. I've always liked spicy foods, ever since I can remember. The heat's never bothered me at all. I just get this really complex layering of spices and flavors, not the heat, not the way everybody else does, I guess. But do you know what I learned when I was reading about being a bird, this week?"

"That technically a bird as big as you can get shouldn't be able to fly?"

Penny laughed. "That too, but no. I learned that birds can't taste capsaicin. The hot stuff in chilis that makes it burn when mammals eat them."

Ashley stared at her, trying to take that in before her jaw dropped. "Wait. Wait, what? You just couldn't taste all of that? *That*'s why you were so sure we could win?"

"'Fraid so. All I tasted were the yummy yummy flavors, not the burning heat."

Ashley burst out laughing and picked Penny up, spinning her around. "Well, aren't you just magnificent!"

"Yes," Penny said modestly. "Also I'm a rock star, did you know that?"

"I *did*. In fact, I'd make you and your bandmate perform for us tonight, but if I do that, I can't dance with you. So we're just going to have to make do with —" Ashley burped and paled. "Excuse me. I have to go to the bathroom again."

"Oh, poor honey! Okay, you go." Penny, eyes sparkling, watched Ashley bolt for the bathrooms, where a woozy-looking Jon was now emerging. Grinning, she made her way over to him. "So that trip to Disneyland…"

Jon groaned with true pathos. "We'll pay up, but can we not talk about it now? I don't know how you're even still standing. You're half my size and you ate twice as many wings. You should be basically dead right now. Laurie's in there lying on the bathroom floor moaning."

Penny giggled. "Small but mighty, you know?"

"What I know is every single bear shifter in this entire family now respects the hell out of you," Jon said wryly. "I mean, they would have anyway, and they would have liked you anyway, because you're Ashley's mate, but damn, woman. You just ate us under the table."

"Good thing it wasn't a drinking contest," Penny

said. "I couldn't have won that. But hot wings, well, I told you I liked them!"

"Yeah, but damn, woman!" Jon grinned down at her a little messily, his stomach still obviously in rebellion. "I think you're good for her, you know? Ash has always been really, I don't know, structured? She wanted things to be just exactly right for everything. Makes her an incredible costumer and amazing at running a business, but she never knows when to step back. Not that I'm saying she should, with getting her feet under her as the manager here, but you're kind of a little chaos in her life, right? I think that's good for her. She can't get so dug into plans and everything having to happen at exactly the right time when your job means you'll be in and out and if she wants to spend time with you, she'll have to adjust to that." He finished, "Oh, God," and ran toward the bathrooms, leaving Penny to laugh after him, and to call, "She's good for me, too!"

Ashley's mom, Holly, came to tuck her arm through Penny's. "Those three are going to be useless for the rest of the night. I'm going to re-introduce you to everybody, since they're all talking about you anyway. Out-eating a bear is once-in-a-lifetime entertainment for these guys."

"I did meet most of them once," Penny protested, slightly embarrassed.

Holly snickered. "Yeah, and if I re-introduce you, you might remember five or ten of their names tomorrow."

By the time Ashley came back out to sway with

Penny on the dance floor, she'd met nearly the entire clan again, and could remember almost a dozen of their names, which would have been more impressive if she hadn't already known about that many.

"It's fine," Ashley whispered into her hair. "You've got lots of time to memorize them. You're perfect, you know? And not just because you can eat capsaicin and put my dumb cousins in their place over that silly beef. You're my dream come true."

Penny grinned. "But putting your cousins in their place didn't hurt, right? How's your tummy?"

"I believe I'm still going to die," Ashley said dramatically. "My bear isn't speaking to me. But," she said with a grin, "we're going to Disneyland, because I'm *fully* gonna make those dorks pay up on that bet, and that'll be awesome."

"Maybe for our honeymoon," Penny said a bit rashly, then felt herself blush as Ashley's eyes widened. "I don't mean to jump the gun. I was just thinking it'd be a great honeymoon."

Ashley's wide eyes turned to a bright smile. "On one hand, yes. On the other, I think the deal Jon suggested was 'the losing team takes the winning team to Disneyland,' and I'm not actually sure I want my cousins along on my honeymoon."

"Oh, God! No! You're right! I hadn't thought of that!" Penny laughed. "Never mind! New plan!"

"We have all the time to make plans." Ashley sealed the promise with a kiss. "And now, because I'm a real romantic, I'm going to beg you to bring me home and tuck me into bed. I still feel awful after all those wings, and if I'm here when the party ends I'll end up staying and supervising until everything's cleaned up."

"My chariot awaits!" Penny said grandly. "If you can accept that I mean 'beat up old van' by 'chariot.'" She put her hand into Ashley's and led her off the dance floor, stopping long enough to collect their coats before they slipped out of the party without saying goodbye. Both of them were asleep by a very sensible hour by rock star standards, although Penny was awakened early by Ashley's quiet giggles and then her phone being slid across the bed toward her.

A long list of text messages were full of admiration and complaint that Ashley had managed to sneak out before cleanup time. Half of them were in support of the two women running off together, but Laurie and Jon were trying to make a new beef of it. Bill had added his two cents, saying, *You're just trying to get out of taking them to Disneyland. Suck it up, bros,* and that had ended the late-night text chain, except for a handful of heart-broken emojis from the two younger brothers.

"This is what you're going to have to put up with forever," Ashley warned Penny sleepily.

"I think I'm getting off easy." Penny reached for her own phone, found a video clip she wanted, and tilted it toward Ashley so she could see a hall full of fans wearing Sixty Pix t-shirts and making an incredible amount of noise as the band came out of an interview. "This is what *you're* going to have to put up with."

"Except *I'm* going to stay away from all of that as

much as possible," Ashley murmured. "*You're* going to keep coming home to my huge crazy family. I think you get the worse end of the deal."

"I absolutely do not," Penny disagreed. "Because I get to spend the rest of my life with you, and there's nothing better I can think of doing."

Ashley gave her a dippy smile and nestled in close. "Well, when you put it that way...oh, Merry Christmas!"

"Yeah," Penny murmured, "yeah. Merry Christmas, always."

CHRISTMAS – ONE YEAR LATER

*P*enny had forgotten about it, when she'd lost the fairy dress on the night of her first shift a year earlier. She'd returned the gown to Karina, the owner of the Looking Glass costume shop, and had been startled to get a call the next day asking if she wanted to come pick up her property. Only then had she remembered sitting down at the drums that night, hitting the cymbals and sending something flying off it and into her hand. She'd barely looked at it, just shoved it in the dress's pocket, and forgotten about it entirely until Karina called.

She'd been holding onto it since, waiting for the right moment. And there weren't a lot of right moments, honestly, not with the Sixty Pix on the road promoting their new album and themselves, not with

Ashley busy expanding the pub's beer garden, not with a hundred family members underfoot all the time. But it was Christmas again, and Penny was determined to make it work somehow.

Mostly by lurking around the pub, hoping Ashley would have a minute to spare. She never did, not with the success of last year's parties to build on. The pub had been booked out for the holidays since March, and Ashley's triumph meant Ashley had to work that much more. Fortunately Penny didn't mind just sitting on a bar stool, beaming when her mate came scurrying through, and generally watching the crowds. But still, she was beginning to think the chance would never arise.

Bill appeared abruptly, energetic and bright-eyed. "Gwen has grabbed Ashley for a minute outside. Go before she slithers away."

Our mate does not slither! She... The partridge went silent immediately, trying to figure out a more delicate word for 'lumbers.' Because bears certainly didn't trip lightly on their toes, dancing through the daisies like... well, possibly like partridges. The partridge was many things, but not clumsy. Lithe and quick, maybe, which also weren't words for a bear. It was still thinking about how to defend Ashley from slither-hood when Penny made it through the throngs and out to the porch where Gwen was chatting with Ash, who was looking guiltily toward the doors and clearly trying to make an escape.

She lit up when Penny came out, though. "I know

you're only here a couple of days, and I'm so sorry it's so crazy busy. It's worse than last year, even without an accidental charity event on the premises." She sounded completely thrilled at that.

Penny, smiling, wrapped her arms around Ashley's waist. "Yes. We fly out in two days for a gig, so I'm going to steal you away for a few minutes because I'm afraid I'll never see you alone if I don't."

"Oh, but I can't," Ashley said unhappily. "The pub—"

"Bill has the pub," Gwen told her. "You can take half an hour with the love of your life and just get off your feet and enjoy yourselves."

Ashley said, "But," as Penny took her hand and dragged her away from the pub.

Gwen yelled, "At least half an hour! More is better!" and went inside.

"You coordinated this, didn't you?" Ashley asked without any real accusation. She was relaxing even if she thought she should be on for the pub 24/7. "You all think I need a break."

"We're all right, too," Penny said. "But since I have to leave in two days and your head would explode if I tried to take you away from the pub during the holidays, I'm going to put off insisting we take two weeks at a hot springs until January." Instead, she brought Ashley to her van, which was one of the least romantic spots she could imagine, but at least it was immediately available. She'd had the engine going on and off all afternoon, keeping it warm, and they both climbed into the back to collapse in a bean bag Penny had thrown in there.

Ashley, despite her protests, groaned as she sank into the beans and let some more tension go. "I could just shift into a bear and sleep here for the rest of the winter," she suggested, not meaning it but sounding like she wished she did. "New pub rule: bean bag lunches. Just a quick nap to perk you up. Hey, where you going?" She made a lazy grab at Penny as she slid off the bean bag, then sat up, amused, as Penny hit the metal floor. "What are you doing?" Then her eyes widened as Penny got herself arranged correctly, down on one knee. "Oh my God, what are you doing?"

"Proposing," Penny said, feeling a little silly. "Obviously."

"Obviously! But oh my God!" Ashley clapped both hands to her face, eyes wide over them. "Really?"

"Yes, really! I have a ring and everything!" Penny dug the ring out of her pocket, which took far more effort than it had the hundred times she'd practiced, and finally managed to get it out and wrench the box top open.

It really was a lovely ring. Gold, inset with flecks of silver and then a trio of diamonds. More of a wedding band than an engagement ring, maybe, but it would do.

Ashley's jaw fell open. "Oh my gosh, Pen. Where did you get that?"

"It's the last of the five golden rings from last year's treasure hunt," Penny whispered. "It was on the cymbal. It flew off when I hit it the first time, and then I had to fix the screw so the cymbals would work, and then I turned into a partridge and forgot all about it. And then I've been saving it since then. I told you I'd find it for you, remember?" She took a deep breath, surprised at how nervous she was.

It's fine, her partridge crooned, reassuring for the first and Penny hoped not last time in its life. *She's our mate. Everything will be wonderful.*

Ashley breathed, "*Penny,*" and Penny thought maybe things would be okay, in fact.

"Will you marry me, Ashley?"

"Of course I will." Ashley threw herself forward, nearly knocking them both backward, then corrected and hauled Penny backward into her lap to kiss her. "Yes, of course I will! Yes! Want to get married tomorrow? On Christmas?"

Penny laughed between kisses, surprised. "Do you think we could find somebody to perform the ceremony?"

Ashley, gleefully, said, "Yes!" and then, dryly, "And then my mother would kill us, because she'll want a whole big shindig. And the rest of the family will want to come. And the Sixty Pix should be there. All of them, not just Gwen."

"Next summer, then." Penny grinned and kissed her mate again. "A little time to plan, but not enough time to go completely overboard."

"I've seen what you can do on a single day's notice," Ashley said. "You can totally go overboard in six months."

"Not if I'm on tour half of it!"

"I bet that wouldn't stop you."

Penny laughed again and nestled close. "You're probably right, but I'll try. Big, small, whatever you want. I'm going to spend the rest of my life as the partridge in your bear tree."

Ashley, sounding genuinely shocked, said, "Penny!" but before she could get any farther, burst into laughter. "I'm not sure I want to marry you anymore, if you're going to say things like that!"

"Yes, you do." Penny stole a kiss, and Ashley ducked her head to rub her nose against Penny's.

"Yeah, I do," she murmured. "C'mon, babe. Let's go tell everybody we're gonna live happily ever after."

"Uh-uh. You've got at least," Penny checked her phone, "seventeen minutes of break time left, and I'm not giving you up for a single one of them."

"In that case." Ashley's voice dropped into that delicious low-pitched purr she had. "I bet I can think of some wonderful things to do for seventeen minutes."

Build a nest? the partridge said hopefully,

Penny giggled. *Yeah. Yeah, that's exactly it.* Aloud, she said, "Read me a phone book?"

"Yes," Ashley said dryly. "Yes, that's exactly what I'm planning. No, wait," she said with a sudden laugh. "No, I have something better to read to you. I was looking for good stuff. Here. Here." She grabbed for her phone, opened a book, and cleared her throat. "You want the back of book blurb first?"

"Yeah," Penny said warily, which was difficult when

she was already laughing. "I think so. I gotta know what I'm getting into."

"All right. All right. Here we go." Ashley cleared her throat again, then put on a radio-announcer movie-trailer kind of voice that sent a shiver right through Penny's bones. "'*The dastardly Corpus Corporation has long known there are shifters among us. What they have never been able to do is command the power that lets a human and a beast share a soul... until now!*'"

Penny said, "Oh my *God*," and sat up. "What is this?"

"I have no idea. I mean, it's a shifter romance. It's a thing. Somebody out there is cashing in—I hope—on us existing, and this has got to make it less likely that anyone would believe that we do, right? Just listen. '*Derek Montague is everything a woman could want—hand-some, wealthy, a brave protector who has done his time as a Navy Seal...but his secret wish has always been to be more. When he's offered a chance to participate in a dangerous new experiment, Derek can't resist the opportunity that could make him able to swim freely in the depths of the sea... the chance to be what no one has been before...the chance to become... SHARK-MAN!*'"

Penny shrieked. "Oh my God. Keep going!"

"I will, if you'll stop interrupting!" Ashley went back to her movie-trailer voice. "*Gorgeous scientist Candice Mallus knows the work she does to develop a new line of corporate-sponsored shifters is borderline unethical— but that's why she will only accept volunteers for the perilous transformations she's trying to trigger. Mixing animal DNA with a man's was sure to have some unintended conse-*

quences, but she never expected love to be one of them. But from the moment Candy lays eyes on Derek, she knows there's something special about him..... more than the successful graft that turns him into the first shifter ever created by humanity.

But Derek's metamorphosis awakens a savage strength within him, and an undeniable rage at the very corporation that has given what he has always desired. Will his new power destroy the hopes of a generation...or can scientific beauty soothe the sharkish beast?'"

Penny clapped her hands over her face. "Yes. Yes, you need to read me this entire book immediately. Right now, please."

"I can't," Ashley said cheerfully. "I have to go back to work in nine minutes. But as soon as we get home tonight..."

"I bet you anything Bill will cover the rest of your shift. I'm kidnapping you home right now."

"You can't—"

Penny already had her own phone out, texting Bill, and a moment later held it up in triumph as he responded with *take her away, I've got the pub for tonight.* "I'm driving. You're reading. It'll be a night to remember."

Ashley put her phone down, took Penny's away, and snuggled her up close. "I'm sure it will be," she murmured, "but it's the lifetime that I'm looking forward to. I love you, Pen."

Warmth and joy spilled through Penny, followed by

a giggle. "I love you, too. My life would be un*bear*able without you."

"Oh my God. No, never mind, this isn't going to work." Ashley made a show of trying to crawl away, but Penny grabbed her and pulled her back for a kiss.

"Yeah, it is. We're *tweethearts*, nothing to be done about it now."

Ashley shouted a protesting laugh, but fell into the kiss, and Penny knew they were going to live happily e*bear* after.

ACKNOWLEDGMENTS

My profound thanks to early readers Susan Baur, Caroline Westra, Carol Guess, Mary Hargrove, Michael Bernardi, Doreen Farrer, Cris Perry, Bryant Durrell, Linda Cox, Kathy Rogers, and Heather Roney for catching numerous typos and other errors in this book! Any other unnoticed mistakes are obviously entirely my own fault.

-Catie

ABOUT THE AUTHOR

Some say Murphy Lawless is the descendant of Irish gangsters, exiled to Australia, who has made good on the family name. It's probably true*.

But then, others claim that Murphy was a spy for the Allies during the war. Stories are told of daring rescues of intrepid reporters from almost certain death, but Murphy has never admitted to anything. Still others say Lawless studied with a local tribe for years after crash-landing in the untamed wilds, having accepted a dare from a pilot of ill repute, and came away from the experience a kinder, wiser, gentler soul.

Even now, though, the most widely held belief is that Lawless left Australia as a mere slip of a thing, and made a fortune in the wilds of the Alaskan oil fields before realizing that romance was the ultimate adventure. Murphy now writes passionate, fun-filled stories of paranormal romance and destined love.

*Probably.

You can find Murphy at catiemurphy.com, Patreon, and at her newsletter, which is by far the best way to have up-to-date information delivered straight to you!